After

After

CLAIRE TRISTRAM

FARRAR, STRAUS AND GIROUX

NEW YORK

Farrar, Straus and Giroux
19 Union Square West, New York 10003

Copyright © 2004 by Claire Tristram
Distributed in Canada by Douglas & McIntyre Ltd.
Printed in the United States of America
First edition, 2004

The passage quoted on page vii is from ghazal 23, as translated
by Elizabeth T. Gray Jr., in *The Green Sea of Heaven: Fifty
Ghazals from the Diwan of Hafiz* (White Cloud Press, 1995).

Library of Congress Cataloging-in-Publication Data
Tristram, Claire.
    After / Claire Tristram.— 1st ed.
        p.   cm.
    ISBN 0-374-10390-9 (hardcover : alk. paper)
    1. Terrorism victims' families—Fiction.   2. Adultery—
Fiction.   3. Muslims—Fiction.   4. Widows—Fiction.
I. Title.
    PS3620.R58A68 2004
    813'.6—dc22   2003021585

EAN: 978-0-374-10390-3

Designed by Debbie Glasserman

www.fsgbooks.com

10   9   8   7   6   5   4   3   2   1

To Bernie Asbell

The threshold of love's sanctuary lies above that of reason. To kiss that threshold you must be ready to scatter your life like coins.

—HAFIZ

After

1

As the anniversary of her husband's death drew near it became clear to her that she needed to get away. His family would call that day, looking to comfort and to be comforted, and discover a woman who was not quite stable. The newspapers would also surely want a quote, some sort of quote, something to give to their readers the kind of cathartic release that only a stoic, grieving widow could provide. But she could no longer be stoic, nor grieving. Day by day, month after month, without her attending to it, her grief had subtly changed its shape, until what was left was not quite grief at all, but something she could only describe as desire. She ate with her fingers. She slept naked. Grocery boys aroused her.

At the end of this cold year she made up her mind to go away with a man. She had seen him first across a trade show floor, had seen him watching her. When they met again that night at one of those dreary-hot convention parties, he had kissed her with the weepy desire of a schoolboy. She, ready, not ready, had sent him away. Only to call him two weeks later. She gave him a date. She picked a hotel on the recommendation of her grief counselor, a place that suited her needs, on the Pacific coast, three hours away from where anyone she knew might find her. I need to get away for a while, she told her agent, who nodded and said, yes, yes, of course, I always told you that you started work too soon.

It was already dark when she reached the hotel, an old, hollowed-out place that had clearly seen better days, set on a cliff overlooking the sea lying exposed, on the headlands, a mile north of the nearest town. The parking lot was empty. She parked near the door and sat in the car, wondering vaguely if there would be a porter. When no one appeared she got out, lifted her heavy bags from the trunk by herself, and wheeled them into the lobby, a cavernous and empty space with a wooden floor, polished dark, and a great stone hearth at its center, blackened from years of use. There was no fire. The back of the lobby, toward the sea, was glass. In the cold dark of early evening the surface looked reflective, like obsidian. The wheels of her bags clattered along the wooden floor. A man at the front desk sat on a revolving stool, watching her progress in silence. He looked up and smiled broadly when she reached him, as if she had surprised him suddenly instead of clattering across the floor with her bags. He made her pay cash. She expected nothing more from him. It seemed lately that fewer and fewer places were willing to accept anything besides hard currency. She took her key and thanked him, and dragged her bags through hallways that seemed to lead off in all directions until she found the door with her number on it. The room itself was clean enough. He would arrive in the morning. She sat down on the edge of the bed, suddenly fatigued. It had taken everything she had in her to get this far. Really, she was proud of herself for following through. It hadn't been easy. But for what? She avoided looking in any of the mirrors. She looked instead at her suitcases by the door, two of them. What could she possibly have brought with her? She didn't remember. She had no will to unpack. She showered, then sat on the bed again, this time wrapped in a towel, listening to the drip of water from the bathroom. They would be calling her. Her mother. Her sisters. Her brother-in-law. She had unplugged the answering machine. Her phone would ring on, and on, and on, and after a while the ones who had called her and received no answer would begin to call each other and ask, Where is she? What has happened?

To distract herself from these thoughts she put her clothes back on and went out of the room again, wandering about the hallways until she found the lobby again, and the dining room. The hostess was too young

for her job. The hostess looked as if she were playing
dress-up, wearing her mother's dress.

"One?" the girl asked.

She nodded, and was led across the dining room, its
walls wrapped in velvet curtains and with not a hint of
sea view, only black reflecting back from the windows
to the west. The hostess stopped at a table for six and
pulled out a chair with a velvet-covered seat.

"I'll just get a menu for you," she said, and went
away.

She sat down and looked around. There were tiny
lamps on each table, their fringed shades a dingy pink.
I have fallen into a film noir, she thought.

The dining room was almost empty. The only others in the room were a man in a business suit and a
much younger woman who were sitting on the same
side of a booth, about a dozen feet away, eating ice
cream and drinking wine. They looked back at her a
moment, then forgot her. The man drunkenly touched
the woman's nose with his spoon, leaving a thick spot
of vanilla. He leaned over and kissed it off. The girl
laughed and tried to pay him back in kind, but he held
her back with a thick-fingered grasp around her wrist.
He grabbed the girl's wrists and kissed her again, this
time on the mouth. The girl made a show of resisting,
then capitulated. Why did she let him do that? So public. So crude. She felt herself flushing and looked away,
to the aquarium near her table. One fish was missing an
eye. Her hunger left her. She wanted to go. She dreaded
the long walk back across the floor.

Two waiters came through swinging kitchen doors, far across the dining room, and now stood with their backs to her, folding napkins on a long table. Their voices carried over the empty room.

"My cousin says every man on the line has the same little red bumps," the shorter one said. "No one can explain it. Little red bumps. Right here. Along the arms."

"Some kind of rash," the tall one said. "I heard it on the radio."

She felt a fluttering panic begin to form in the center of her chest. Should she try to catch their attention with a cough, then gesture for a menu? To walk over to them? To go back to the room again? She should have stayed at home. She should have chosen one of the grocery boys. Not this elaborate plan that in the end would be equally sordid and pointless. Suddenly agitated, she stood up, her chair scraping the bare floor and filling the room with anxious sound. The lovers looked up from their ice cream. The waiters looked up from their napkins. She stood there and watched the shorter one make his way toward her, smiling.

"How can I help you?" he said.

She sat down again.

"I would very much like to know what the specials are tonight," she said, and flushed at how pained she sounded, how near tears.

"Of course. The specials."

He hurried away, back toward the kitchen. Maybe he needed to ask the cook about the specials. She sat down. The lovers in the booth rose to go. The thick-fingered man's hand rested on the back of his young lover's neck as they walked.

"Fuck that Cesar, fuck him," she heard him say as he passed.

The man's language did not match his tone, which sounded as flat and emotionless as a recorded message that had been rewound and played over and over again. He caressed the back of his lover's neck. She watched them and wondered what to make of it. The couple passed from her sight. She looked down at the table-cloth in front of her. She touched the flatware. She had always found it difficult to know where to put her eyes when she dined alone.

The waiter returned with a menu.

"There are no specials tonight, ma'am," he said.

She ordered a salad and some tea. The price of the salad was exorbitant but she felt a craving for fresh, raw vegetables and was willing to pay for them. As she ate she thought about kisses, and rashes. She really knew nothing at all about the man who was coming to meet her. Nothing. He had the face you might see these days in the pages of any newspaper. The deep-set eyes. The youthful, fawn-colored skin. The skin of a martyr. She tried to imagine what she would have done if her husband had tried to kiss her in the manner of her future lover, the man she would see tomorrow.

But her husband was dead, and she could not imagine it.

2

Later, in her room again, made anxious by the dank whispers rising up from the sea, she found herself falling into a familiar, restless melancholy, a loneliness so desperate and black that she felt as if she were falling into a yawning maw. To save herself she opened cabinets and drawers until she found what she was looking for, some hotel stationery, mildewed but serviceable. She arranged herself on a chair, happy to have purpose again, and pulled herself up to the cramped writing desk in the corner. She held the pen tightly, eager to begin, then put it down again. What was left to write? What was possibly left to write? Her fingers traced bleached white rings in the wood left from someone else's drinks, and she found herself thinking of the other restless and ugly meetings that had occurred here, here in this very room, and she felt less lonely than before. She sat a long time, and then, at last, she began.

"Darling," she wrote, and crossed it out, because she had never called him that when he was alive.

"Honey. Hon. Last night I was watching a cooking show on television and the chef lifted a fork and fed his guest something messy and sweet, and I began to cry. There is no one lifting a fork in my direction these days. I can't seem to forget how much you mean to me. My grief counselor said I must write you all down. I'm not sure if it is a purgative exercise or a redemptive one. These days I usually do what I'm told without questioning it much.

"Well then. I will leave out hurt or exalted feelings, revelations, sentimentalities, peak erotic experiences, and other turning points. All of these things I have covered already, and really they are the very things I am least likely to forget. They have a way of enduring even without extraordinary measures. It's the everyday events that are in danger of falling apart. I remember the avocado. The only seed we ever succeeded in coaxing to grow after being impaled with toothpicks and set on a windowsill. We watched it daily, our simple miracle. Eventually we planted it in the front yard. We did a ridiculous amount of digging for such a small plant. It was a late-summer afternoon. We dug until our fingernails were full of dirt. A child in the neighborhood was playing a piano by an open window. I think it must have been a child because I remember the same few seconds of tune repeated over and over again, leading up each time to the same mistake, after which 'Chopsticks' is played; and just at one of those moments, precisely at the beginning of 'Chopsticks,' our neighbor comes along on the sidewalk, that fellow who was so many decades older than we were, you know, ancient, the one who used to power-walk past the house with weights in his hands. Only this time he didn't have his weights. He stopped in front of our house and cleared his throat until we were looking at him—he had to cough to catch our attention because we never did learn one another's names—and he said, 'Oh, look at you two. Don't you two look like opera buffs. I have two tickets to *Fidelio* that I'm trying to give away.' He held the tickets out. And even though you never thought about opera before or since, your sense of honor was pricked by his unnecessary largesse, and you said, 'Oh, of course we will pay you for them.' And after some back-and-forth you took your wallet out of your back pocket and paid him and he went away, never to be seen again without his weights, and there you were, tickets in your dirt-covered hands, smiling at me, as happy as if you had won an office football pool, and we barely had time to shower off the dirt and get dressed and drive into the city, where we sat in the highest balcony and watched an opera where a wife helps her husband break out of prison, all that drama far below us, so breathtakingly far below that I felt as if I might tumble down onto the stage, and the whole time you rested your hand on my right thigh. Hon, I think I must have chosen this memory for its sequence of serendipitous events, beginning with a fertile avocado pit. I see now that in those days I lived in a world where every event was connected in some lucky and happy way with what had come immediately before, in an unbroken string leading all the way back to early childhood. It's a way of ordering the world that works quite well as long as nothing comes along to challenge it. I still mostly find myself thinking along these lines, even now. But see how much I must have skipped over. That night we must have showered together, because there wasn't time for anything else. You may have washed my back. You may have zipped my dress for me. You enjoyed simple married intimacies of this sort. I can't remember. We must have taken the steps two by two, holding hands, running up the stairs to make it to our seats in time. There were other staircases I walked with you, too, at other times, like those ancient stone steps we ascended near Cancún, also hand in hand, also with you leading me and going so fast I thought I would never find my breath again. See, how my mind insists on making connections between two events that have no causal relationship whatsoever, except that they are memories involving steps. That day we had grown bored with the Cancún beaches and hired a car and drove west, into the jungle, in search of ruins. We found them easily, big pyramids stacked by the side of the only road, surrounded by crumbling adobe buildings of a much later vintage. The whole area looked like a cheap roadside attraction

rather than the real thing. The Mexicans seemed to be
in on the scam. Two boys came from nowhere and held
up an iguana the moment we got out of the car. It was
as large as the smaller of the two boys, the one who was
holding up the iguana's tail. You wanted to be kind to
them. You would tell me later how difficult it must be
to be a Mexican boy with nothing but an iguana to sell.
I remember thinking, Thank God I'm here or my husband would probably buy that lizard out of pity. The
air was hot and crowded with the sound of screaming
insects. A bus full of Florida retirees arrived, sending
up a cloud of dust in front of us. We fell in with them
as we marched along the path toward the ruins. Two
women just ahead were complaining of the heat. Their
husbands walked just behind, practicing their Spanish:
Una cerveza, por favor. Una mas, por favor. Followed by
much backslapping between the two. I have noticed
over the years that men do a great deal of backslapping
in youth and old age. Then a loner in Bermuda shorts
began to walk in stride with us. He seemed to consider
us part of the attraction. He asked us all sorts of personal details about our marital status and drug use,
stemming from his precise and unshakeable ideas about
young American couples he had come across in Mex-
ico. You increased our pace and he fell behind. You led
me to the base of a stone pyramid where we began to
climb the steps as if we were escaping from a crisis. We
climbed until we left even the most fit of those geriatric
Floridians behind us and were alone again. The steps
grew very tall. I was suffering from the tempo you set

for us. Eventually we ascended into that perfect blue-white haze that you see only when climbing up to the highest place around on a cloudless day, and we had nowhere left to climb, so we sat down. You put your arm around me. We sat a long time, watching arrangements of people below, watching the tops of their heads coming together in groups of twos, threes, sixes, before falling away and rearranging themselves. All we could hear up there was the wind. It wasn't a strong wind. Nevertheless, in that silence, it filled the ears and drowned out all incidental noise, and it left me, somehow, with the calm certainty that our lives had meaning and structure. I thought deeply about the others who had sat there in the past, on this very spot where we sat, and who had heard the very same wind in their ears. Tourists from Japan. Sacrificial virgins. And now us, an ex-Catholic and a Jew who loved one another and who were sharing this moment with one another. In spite of our many differences, just at that moment I felt connected with you and with all the world, all the way back to beginning times. I felt that we understood one another absolutely, that we were breathing from the same body and thinking the same thoughts. After a while you spoke. You mentioned that you'd had scenes from Stanley Kubrick's *Full Metal Jacket* on your mind ever since we'd gotten up that morning. You couldn't understand it. Why of all things was Stanley Kubrick's *Full Metal Jacket* stuck in your mind? You supposed it must have been the feeling of being in a foreign country, far from home, where the customs were not known.

Your comment precipitated an argument. I walked down alone. At the base of the pyramid I bought a green soapstone necklace. I waited for you at the car. You took your time about it.

"And now, hon, what I am remembering is the last time we were together. I came back from work first and had lain down on our bed for what I thought was a brief, still moment, not bothering to change out of my clothes. I had a plan to get up in a few minutes and fix dinner. Really, I don't think I even took my shoes off. I used my hand for a pillow instead of the real pillow, because I had every intention of getting up. But I fell asleep. I'm sorry. I'm so very sorry. You were going away early in the morning and had to work late that night to prepare for the trip, and by the time you came home I was dead asleep, but I woke up enough that I felt you undress me, slowly, sweetly, rolling me over and pulling off my clothes as you would a little child who has fallen asleep, until I was completely naked, and still I was feigning sleep because I was very, very tired, and I wasn't wanting you in that way. I could feel the heat of you as you leaned over me. I heard a catch in your breath. But I was very tired and I acted like a dead person, until you sighed, and covered me up gently with the blankets and lay down next to me and put your arm around my middle. You fell asleep before I did, and we did not make love that night, and now it is very dark here, my dear love, and late, it is too late for me to remember any more."

She put the pen down and climbed into the bed, but

carefully, not wanting to disturb the neat folds, the perfection of this bed. For the first time she noticed how she still slept to one side, as if waiting for him. She felt the coldness of the sheets, and felt the terror of his absence, and it dawned on her that she had forgotten his face entirely.

3

He sat in the bleachers of the gymnasium of the high school, watching his daughter's volleyball game with his wife at his side. Shouts glittered from the walls. Someone's knees pressed into his back. His own knees were brushing the back of the man sitting in front of him. Before they had left that night his wife had pinned a ribbon to his shirt. She wore one herself, as did the others in the stands with them. Small loops of ribbon. Different colors. They all had one. He squeezed his wife's hand. This other thing, his plan for tomorrow, was there in his mind but not there, not in words really, more like a phantom thrill that traveled up from his groin to his head and then released itself in a kind of shiver, a fleeting terror, a shift in the light around his head. He was grateful to be in a place where he could periodically shout and slap at his knees without being out of place.

He looked at the woman beside him now, his wife, his own wife, luxuriating next to him in the posture of a long-happily-married woman, and thought of the shapes of the other women's breasts he had once known. The breasts of the first woman he had bedded, he remembered still, had a lumpiness to them that always gave the impression that he was caressing a cloth bag filled with marbles. Others had the touch of soft pastry. One woman had told him before she undressed that she had implants, a concept he found both fascinating and repulsive; her breasts had felt like nothing more than fine leather upholstery. And then there were genitalia in all their varieties: some flat and efficient; others voluminous mounds of Venus reaching up toward him and bumping into him as they coupled. He thought of each of these women, one by one, and tried to decide whether the shape and feel of each woman's privates betrayed her inner life in any way. When he was young he had imagined that women would continue to come to him, ceaselessly and without particular effort on his part. Instead, women apart from his wife had stopped paying attention to him just after the crisis in his country had come to a satisfactory conclusion, after Americans were out of danger once more. Overnight he had lost his mystery and his aura of the forbidden and had become bland, unattractive, sexless.

Until this woman, his future lover, had plucked him out of a crowd at the trade show and made him feel desirable again. He had first taken her to be some sort of business executive. She was dressed in a suit; a fine, businesslike navy suit. She laughed and told him, no, she was an actress, a kind of actress at least, not much of one, oh, a commercial here and there when she was younger, but mostly what she did was give speeches in trade show booths, presentations where she often didn't understand the products or what she was selling people. She held no grudges against the world. She was good at her job. People believed her in the role. She was much in demand. It wasn't what she had expected in life, but then, whatever is? He was moved by her speech. She seemed to embrace her fate. He had never met an actress before. Before they kissed he asked her if she was married. She told him no, but in a way he found unconvincing. She was awkward and blushed easily, unskilled in playing the part of unfaithful lover. Never mind. He would learn her secrets. He showed her pictures of his wife and children from his wallet, and as he did so he wondered if it was a ritual that other married men had followed before. The ceremonial picture-showing. He could not be the first. He supposed there were rules to this sort of thing. Perhaps this woman knew the rules. Just then, as she looked at his little collection of family snapshots, her blushes had fallen away and she had looked very assured of herself. Perhaps her lack of a convincing answer about a husband was part of the act. She glanced through them, then handed them back, no longer interested. By this time, only a few minutes into their first conversation, her smallest gesture had the power to move him. Her name had sounded somehow familiar to him. Had she been in some movie or play he may have heard of? No, no. She waved off his question, looking embarrassed. Later when she was allowing him to press himself against her body and to feel her breasts beneath her blouse, it hardly mattered to him why she seemed so familiar; she was a woman. After they parted her name continued to follow him about in his mind, like a small cloud. He searched his wife's stacks of old magazines until he found what he was seeking: her face, her name, a photo of her standing at a microphone surrounded by people holding candles. Her face was apricot-colored, lit by the candlelight and the inner glow of stoic bravery. How different from that hot and wild face he had kissed in the dark! And yet the same. Then her motives had seemed simple. Now that he knew who she really was, her motives had become terribly complicated. It was the way of things, order into chaos. And yet knowing her to be so afflicted, to be a widow under these extreme circumstances, made her infinitely more precious to him. He wondered whether this widow had sensed in him also a gap, a hole, a tragedy in need of resolution and healing, just as he had somehow sensed it in her. Her hair was dark, not blonde as he had imagined the hair of an illicit lover in his fantasies. Her breasts were small. She was wiry and muscular, like a young boy. She must have recognized him as a fellow sufferer. Such people are marked, he had long thought. They could locate one another in a crowd based on instinct

alone. She had recognized him. That was it. He stood
with the magazine in his hand and rubbed the face in
the photograph with his thumb, trying to discern underneath the face of the woman he had known. Then
he put the magazine away carefully and did not look at
it again.

And then she had called him. At his home, breath-
lessly indiscreet, she had called him and they had made
a plan, even as his daughters argued with one another
somewhere in a dim corner of the house and his wife
loaded clothes into the washing machine, working just
on the other side of an open door from the kitchen
where he stood. He had answered the phone casually,
expecting it to be the friend of one of his daughters,
then stood there, transfixed by her voice, unprepared
for her voice, watching the second hand revolve around
the face of the kitchen clock on the wall, needing to
look somewhere tangible lest his wife or daughters appear and find him staring back at them with guilt rav-
aging his face. A plan was made. And ever since he had
been living in two bodies: one that carried on this normal life, and one that felt faint at the sight of anything
beautiful; a leaf, a bird, his wife, his daughter just now
reaching for the volleyball on the court below him.
Each moment seemed both inexpressibly lovely and
threatening to his well-being.

He would see her tomorrow.

His wife noticed a friend in the bleachers above
them and stood up to wave: *How are you?* she mouthed.
She was the only woman who wore lipstick and a skirt
to her daughter's games. She sat down again, her hip

nudged more closely to him than before, and gave him
a look he couldn't interpret. Could she know? Could
she possibly know? A whistle, a forked cry, and all
stood again as a girl diving for a ball missed and did
not get up. The others huddled around the injured
girl. The coach came running out. After some harried
consultation—Is it the ankle? Can you stand? The girl
stood, leaning on her coach, and hopped off the court.
Those in the bleachers clapped briefly and sat down.
The game went on. His daughter looked stern, concentrating on the task of winning. Now and then she
would glance surreptitiously up to where her parents
sat, at her mother especially, whom she pitied. To their
daughter they would always be foreigners. His wife's
lips, lipstick, dark red, moved as she leaned over to say
something to him that he couldn't hear. She used
makeup as redemption, as emancipation. She never
went without it. A *hijab* had never touched her head. In
some ways she was more beautiful than the one he was
going to see.

Alas, his daughter's team did not prevail. On the way
home she cried quietly in the back seat.

"I don't see why you are crying," his wife said. "It's
only a game. You played your best. That's what matters."

It was unclear to him, as it often was, whether his
wife believed her own platitudes or simply wanted
their daughter to believe them.

"Tell her," she said to her husband. "Please speak
with your daughter."

He tried to appreciate his wife's words; his daughter's tears. He found them both incomprehensible, part

of a life from which he had already separated himself. He was thinking about the next day. About the touch of the widow. About her hands inside his shirt. It occurred to him, slowly, that his wife was waiting for him to say something.

"It's only a game," he echoed. "You played your best."

It seemed to satisfy them both.

"Tomorrow I'm keeping the girls home from school," his wife announced. "I don't think you should be traveling. It's not a good day for traveling. It would be better for everyone if you just told them you can't make it. They are always doing this, asking you to do the things no one else will do."

Her hand fluttered at his hair, his collar. He brushed her away, smiling, still looking at the road.

"Tomorrow will be a very good day for traveling," he said.

"You of all people should know how things can change from one moment to the next," she said.

He did. Nevertheless, just as he had with his wife's hand, he brushed her comment away in his mind with studied forgetfulness.

That night she lay in bed with her back curved away from him, still irritated at his refusal to accede to her wisdom. But she did not object when he rested his arm over her. She was lumpy and sweet, and warm, like a pear. He loved her.

He fell asleep easily, dreaming nothing.

4

She had seen a grief counselor, of course. Her husband's company paid for it. The counselor was a beige sort of woman, with hair that matched the freckles on her face and arms. She invariably wore a dress of shapeless tan crepe. The counselor always leaned forward in her seat, fixing her sallow eyes on the face of her patients in a way that telegraphed myopia rather than concern. Almost as if she were searching for her spectacles and not really listening at all. Nevertheless, the counselor had given her hope. She had even given her something to do. She was to write her feelings down every day in a journal. Lately these writings had transformed themselves into letters. She had discovered that she could tell her husband things she had never spoken of when he was alive, now that he was no longer around to interrupt, to console, to make her feel some other way.

"How do you feel?" the grief counselor had asked.

She wanted to answer. There had to be an appropriate answer in these sorts of situations. She didn't want to be overly emotional; rather, she hoped to give a reasoned response, something that would aid the counselor in helping her. She turned her attention inward, closing her eyes, as much to get away from the counselor's felicitous stare as to investigate the fabric of her feelings. How did she feel? She heard her own voice in her head shouting, Oh shame, oh shame on you, is there no shame in you? over and over again. The voice probably had something to do with the peculiar situation in which she found herself: a young widow in a country full of people who wanted to help her. People like her brother-in-law, for instance, who coincidentally a few days earlier had kissed her on the mouth—which, after all, was only the custom on his side of the family, but in this particular instance the brother-in-law had allowed the slightest, most fleeting pressure from his tongue to rake across her lips, even in a room full of their mutual relatives, and the message had been unmistakable, it said, Yes, I know you're grieving, and believe me, whatever you need, I am here to help; and she had felt her body respond, which had left her with this pernicious residue of shame that bled through and left its stain on any other thought. Come to think of it, her brother-in-law had something of the coloring of this grief counselor, with light brown hair and eyes and a splash of freckles across the bridge of his nose. He had been in her thoughts too much and too often for her own good, and for some reason he had taken to stalking her in real life as well. Oh, not stalking, really! That was far too strong a word for it. But buying her groceries, certainly. Dropping by to see if she needed an errand run, or something fixed in the house, or some man's job done for which he could be of service. All the while looking disconcertingly like his dead brother. Nothing had been said between them. Nothing needed to be said, after the tongue. His unflagging niceness made all generous acts from any quarter seem sullied with a pornographic cheapness. His wife, proud homemaker with spotless counters, would invite her over for the Sabbath, then would come over on odd days to clean and run errands, and she was just as cheerfully generous with her husband, urging him to do his best to see the poor widow through these rough times. The wife had found herself through adherence to the religious ritual, and had subsequently lost the will to acknowlede any unpleasantness that might creep into her daily life. Or perhaps she was simply tired of her husband's wet and needy urges and wanted nothing more than that he soil someone else's sheets for a change. It was difficult to say.

"Say anything," said the grief counselor.

She watched the grief counselor's hands gently clasp and unclasp, and thought about all the other people in

pain that had graced this couch, with the grief counselor sitting across from them. The counselor leaned
forward and squinted, waiting for a reply.

"I feel oppressed by all things beige," she answered.

The grief counselor's hands ceased their rhythmic
clasping and unclasping.

"What does beige mean to you?" she said.

"You know. Beige. Tan. Off-white."

"Go on."

"Skin," she said. "Soiled sheets."

A manic exhilaration overtook her.

"Hair. Semen. Sand. Dirty teeth. Bacon grease."

"Very good," the counselor said. Nevertheless, the
counselor had arranged an exceedingly blank look on
her face, as if she knew she was being toyed with. Or
perhaps, being a counselor instead of a therapist, she
merely found these deeper psychological associations
outside of her realm of expertise and wanted to avoid
making any comment about them in case she led her
patient astray.

"Very, very good," the counselor said. "I want to
hear more about those feelings next week."

She nodded and smiled back. "Thank you," she said,
"thank you very much indeed," and got up and left the
room, closing the door behind her, walking through a
waiting room of women with used tissues in their
hands, on past the ladies' room and down the hall until
she got all the way to the elevator bank, around a corner, out of sight, where her breathing began to come
in long and ragged gasps—was she about to cry, or to

laugh? She did both, but only after the elevator doors had closed behind her and she had begun falling toward the ground floor.

In their last scheduled session together, the session in which all of her problems were to be magnificently resolved into some happy chord, the counselor had asked her whether she had thought about beginning a new relationship.

"A relationship?" she had asked.

"Yes. A relationship."

"A relationship. Oh yes. Oh my, yes, indeed. I'm thinking about taking a Muslim lover," she said.

She said it to get a rise out of this woman, to be perverted, to be perverse. But maybe not entirely. Even then she wasn't sure of herself. She felt close to some truth. The blank look answered her. The grief counselor had been trained to withhold judgment, and trained very well. The edges of her eyelids seemed to move apart, as if she were repressing a blink.

"Do you think that's a healthy course?" the grief counselor said.

An intense irritation rose up in her. She had come to understand some things would never be put right again. At any rate she had no wish to piece herself together. The cracks would always show. She would never be her old self. This grief counselor and all the others expected her to become clay again, when she was air. What was wise in such a situation? She wondered what her husband would have answered. Not that he would have debased himself to even attend such a session. Oh, he was strong, strong. Stronger than she. The strong one.

"Oh, stop this nonsense," she said. "You and I will never see one another after this hour is done. There is really very little reason to pretend that the wisdom of my choices is of any concern to you."

She immediately regretted her words. She imagined they would hurt the counselor's feelings and cause the counselor to doubt herself and her motives for choosing this line of work, work where she was constantly required to manufacture false attachments with emotionally damaged individuals. To have the bitter, iron hopelessness of her profession thrown back in her face by a patient! It must have been hurtful. She regretted causing pain of this sort. And yet, look: the counselor was positively joyful, with a sticks-and-stones sort of vindication spread out across her bland features! She was impenetrable! She could not be made to suffer!

"It's natural to feel that way," the grief counselor said. "But of course your progress will always be something I will continue to wish for. We're all on the same journey."

It was so clearly the wrap-up speech that there was nothing left to be done but shake the grief counselor's hand, and feel the counselor pull her into a warmly felt hug, and to thank her, and to wish her well.

Nevertheless, the idea of taking a Muslim lover continued to rub at her mind. To do something so unexpected, so clearly outside the role that she had been forced into by her circumstances! The thought became a habit, a harmless fantasy, yet one so deeply hidden, even from herself, that it would startle her anew when she caught herself looking at a dark-skinned man. Any of them. In the library. At the mall. At work. She never spoke to these men. Nor did she mention them in her letters to her husband, which she continued to write dutifully long after her sessions with the counselor had ended. The men, her thoughts about them, meant nothing.

And then he came to her.

5

The next morning, on his long drive alone to meet his future lover, he fell back into the familiar places in his mind and remembered. A memory had followed him for decades now, like a chronic pain, something that had become so natural it became almost bearable, and after becoming bearable, could almost be forgotten. A warm September afternoon when he was a young man, so young that he was still not used to calling himself a man at all. He was carrying a handmade sign and walking in a crowd of young men like himself to a square in the city, where this particular crowd of young men was met by military police. Noth-

ing could compare with the absolute blue of that afternoon. Whenever he remembered that day he first
made himself remember that joy, just before the violence began. He made himself recall the concrete
awareness he had felt, of warm life coursing through
his veins, a feeling so vital that it filled his limbs with an
intensity of purpose he now imagined must have been
rapture. But that part of the memory may have been
added later, layer by layer, until what really happened
and what he remembered happening were insinuated
with each other beyond all reckoning. It was impossible to say how the memories of that afternoon had
evolved over the years, through the many times he had
gone over it, second by second, trying to understand
what other outcomes might have occurred. Walking by
his side on that day was his best friend, a tall, reedy boy
with thick black glasses who was studying aeronautics.
The two of them were not seriously political. It was the
place, however, and the moment to be carrying a sign.
Great changes were in the air and filling their lungs
with exaltation. Then shots came, although even that,
he reminded himself, was a revision of memory; in fact
what he heard was a series of pops that at that moment
had no precise meaning to him. And then his friend
was on his back in the dirt. His friend's hands continued to open and close for a moment. Sometimes he
also thought he remembered that his friend's spectacles were still perched on his nose, although now a bit
askew. Lately, however, he had begun to doubt that his
friend had ever worn spectacles at all. In those few moments his country was forever lost to him, although

this fact, too, impressed itself on his understanding only slowly, over the course of years. Really the only memory he was absolutely sure of, across these many years, was this: the precise movements of his friend's hands as he lay in the dirt. These tiny bits of memory had followed him about like a third child, a child far older, and more antagonistic to him, and more intimately connected with him, than his two daughters ever were. He was profoundly aware of how even these scraps of memory dragged on him, diminishing his sense of life; how they had caused him to become the cautious, morbid sort of man he had loathed in his youth. Since that day in the square he had done research. He tried to understand what had happened from a more objective perspective, to realize the events of that day did not revolve around him alone. It was difficult. In documents written of that time, the truth was muddled with facts, and the facts were not to be trusted. Some sources said hundreds died that afternoon. Others said sixty-eight. He was sure of only one.

By this time, over two hours into his journey, his ruminations on the past had almost obliterated any thought of the future, and the woman he was traveling to meet was barely part of his understanding. A quick turning in the road and he was driving along the sea, a vast expanse of gray upon gray far below. The road clung to the cliff. The sudden opening of the horizon swept his nostalgia along in another direction entirely. His first real memory of the sea was when his family had gone to the Caspian when he was just a young boy. The journey took hours, a winding, tortuous pilgrimage over the mountains on a single-lane road barely etched into the sides of steep cliffs. His mother—how he had loved her!—had bundled him between two older sisters in back before taking her place next to his father, who was a gracious man except when he was behind the wheel of his car. On this day for some reason his father took delight in playing chicken with truck drivers and other motorists, honking his horn in cacophonous abandon as he took up more than his share of the road. His father seemed to take pleasure in taunting his own family, steering as close as he could to the precipice as they rounded the hairpin turns, until the boy wept and closed his eyes and leaned away from the chasm, thinking perhaps that his weight in counterbalance might make the difference between life and death. His father had laughed. An occasional hulking wreck of a car or truck lined the road or punctuated the crevasses below, adding to the boy's terror and conviction that they would meet the same fate. Then came the Kandavan Tunnel. A few seconds into that yawning mouth and all heat and daylight disappeared, and the boy was entombed in a perverse cold that seeped into his skin. At last came a glimmer of hope and daylight, and they spilled out onto the other side, where everything was sun and green, and alive; and then the sudden sea. As a grown man, looking back on that day, he could see in his mind's eye that the beach itself was nothing special. Any view of it was all but blocked by concrete walls painted in garish pinks and greens. The waves barely lapped at the shore. The water itself was a disappointment, the color of beer, with a layer of foam on top. But the boy had been

filled with exultation, running along that strand, overcome by the simple truth that he was still alive; that he
had survived the journey and he was still here, and that
the sea was here to meet him. As he ran along the water and found himself thinking that he was in control of
the ebb and surge at his feet; that his arm movements
alone were shaping the course and rhythm of the waves,
all the way from where they washed over his feet to the
most distant shore; to Russia itself. He was certain he
could stop the repeatable pattern of the waters, should
he choose to do so, with the smallest gesture of his hand.
He did not test his belief only because he was certain of
it. He required no test. A foolish childhood fancy that
had faded as quickly as it came, only to come again as
memory, and to make him wonder how the years and
hours had circumscribed his belief in himself, his capacity to feel. It was not until he was dangerously low
on fuel that he allowed himself to rise up again out of
his reverie and think of something else.

6

Along this stretch of road by the sea the towns were few and the gas stations evidently non-existent. How could he have been so stupid as to have nearly run out of fuel? He turned onto the shoulder of the road to consult a map.

With the engine off his tension diminished. At least he wasn't using up the small amount of fuel left to him. The wind buffeted his car. The engine pinged and sang. He unfolded the map slowly, trying to delay the moment when he ran out of hope of ever reaching her. There had been army trucks now and then. A bus. Surely he would be lucky and someone would come by quickly who could give him a ride to a station. He could still make it. The map was now flat, resting on the steering wheel. He traced the route from him to her with his finger.

Seventy miles at least.

He would never make it.

A car drove by, traveling north. Too late, he thought, to flag it down and ask for help.

He did not know what to do. He looked out and saw to the right, outside his window to the west, that there was a vast cultivated field, with rows of spiky leaves thrusting themselves up through lines of dirt, beyond which sunlight glinted on the sea. He could see a man on a tractor on the other side of the field, kicking up a plume of yellow-brown dust. Farther off a ragged line of men labored in the dirt with baskets on their backs and scarves over their mouths and noses.

Desperate, he turned the engine over and began to drive over the dirt road that skirted the field, making his way toward the tractor, an ever-expanding banner of dust trailing behind his car and announcing his coming. The car bounced over the deep ruts in the dirt. A rhythmic waver began in the front suspension, which increased in amplitude as he progressed, until he felt as if he were at sea. When he came closer, as close as he could come on the road, the tractor pulled around to meet him, until it was in front of the car and blocked his forward movement. He turned off the engine and stepped out. He thought he could feel the dust embedding itself in his skin and hair. He coughed, and noticed dully that the man in the tractor sat with a shotgun resting across his knees. His fingers were not on the trigger, at least. He smiled up at the man.

"I'm sorry to trouble you," he called out. He stood by his car, not advancing further. "I seem to have run nearly out of gas. I'm wondering if you might have any to sell."

The man on the tractor squinted. His entire face seemed to be arranged, with its wrinkles, in a perpetual struggle to guard itself against harsh sunlight and the requests of strangers. The gun rested on his lap. The line of men with baskets on their backs and kerchiefs over their faces labored on, across the field, in a fitful, broken line, bending and picking, bending and picking, men who would have watched any violence with dull eyes, not involving themselves. He stood there and felt the dust blowing all about him and marveled at the strength of his will. Facing a man with a shotgun across his lap felt only natural to him. Having come this far, having thought this long about a woman, he would not be defeated. He smiled again.

"I can pay you well for it," he said.

"Twenty dollars a gallon."

"Beg pardon?"

"Twenty dollars a gallon."

A protest rose up in his chest; he quelled it.

"All right," he said.

The man started his tractor and began to drive back down the road along the field. He got back into his car and followed. The yellow dust kicked up by the tractor fell over his windshield and gave him the impression he was driving through a conflagration. Every once in a

while the man's head and hat would appear through the
haze. He took it as a sign of hope. But when they
reached the main road the man on the tractor turned
north, in the opposite direction of where he wanted
to go. He pushed away his impatience and followed,
crawling along behind at tractor speed, expecting at
any moment to hear his engine sputter and die. Four
miles later the man on the tractor turned off the high-
way, onto a single-lane road that led over a hill to a
house and barn, where they stopped.

He stepped out of the car and followed the man to
the barn. The abrupt change in light from dazzling sun
to the dim interior of the barn blinded him momentarily before he saw long lines of rusting five-gallon cans,
packed high on the side of the barn on sagging wooden
shelves. The dirt floor of the barn was otherwise
empty. Hoarding, he thought. Bootleg rates. Probably
watered down. So it begins. One day, a fire, such a fire
as this hillside has never seen. Never mind. Pay the
man.

The farmer reached a gaunt hand for one of the
cans, and carried it out to the car. The other arm still
carried the gun, but in a relaxed manner, pointing it
low and resting it in the crook of his elbow as if he were
returning from a leisurely duck hunt.

"How much you need?"

"Five gallons."

"I'll gas it for you."

The farmer took the gas cap off, now unexpectedly
helpful. As he did so, his eyes strayed over the bumper
sticker that his wife had pasted to the back of his car,

one with *Proud to Be an American* written in bold blue letters next to an American flag. An outsized, vulgar thing. The farmer's eyes wavered a moment. Then a bright light fell on his face, the wrinkles rearranging themselves into a not entirely reassuring smile.

"Yes sir," the farmer said. "You get an extra gallon for that."

And so his wife, with her ever-solicitous tending to his safety, had helped him along to an adulterous meeting at a distant hotel, with a woman she would have disliked intensely, were the two ever to meet.

7

He was late. She would not stay in the room like some stable animal to wait for him. No.

She dressed quickly, not stopping to brush her hair. She walked through the hotel to the lobby, where she stepped out a back door and ran across a stretch of lawn, still wet from dew, to the very end where the waves crashed below her and an iron staircase was bolted to the side of the cliff. The railing seemed too low to her, as if forcing her to stoop as she descended, to be awkward, to feel as if she might be blown off entirely.

It was colder than it had looked from her room. The sun was thin, barely warm enough, and the wind whipped at her jacket as if trying to rip it from her. She found a red silk scarf in her jacket pocket and tied it around her head. A mother with her small son and daughter were making their way up the staircase, wearing wet bathing suits and clutching towels around themselves, chattering to one another in some foreign language or another. What were they doing swimming in this weather? Some half-baked idea of swimming in the sea must have spurred them on. They must have come from a landlocked country. Travel was so difficult these days. So risky. No doubt they wanted to do everything they could to enjoy the time they spent here, while they still could. But still. The children were shaking with the cold. She pressed herself against the cliff to let them pass. The little girl was sucking on some sort of plastic toy. The girl frowned at her as she climbed by, as if accusing her of some transgression. After they had passed she hurried down the rest of the stairs to the sand. The beach had the air of vacant fairgrounds. Trash scuttled across the sand before getting stuck in clumps of seaweed. The tide was out, receding, flowing away from her. A few gulls followed her listlessly, looking for food. Otherwise the beach was empty of life. The only footprints on the sand were those of the three who had just passed her on the stairs. No boat passed along the horizon. The sand beneath her feet was deep and dry and shifted with each step. She walked closer to the water, to the tide line, to find her footing. One of the gulls dove close and shrieked at her, then banked away. The sound of its cry, grief-filled, accusing, seemed to wrap itself in a melancholy way around her mind. Do gulls mourn? she thought. It was hard to imagine their dull minds occupied with more than the next meal. That is what separates us from the animals, she thought. We understand the pity of it all. She listened to the rasp of her feet treading on the sand and looked back over her shoulder, to where she had just walked, and was grateful to see the unbroken line of her footprints where a wave had not yet reached. She resolved to think of her husband. It was right that she should be thinking of her husband. Instead of the familiar grief, she found herself frustrated, unable to think of him for more than the most fleeting moments, a memory that she couldn't quite catch, like these bits of trash blowing along the sand. "I loved you," she whispered. She said it over and over again, with each step, because after all there was no one to hear her.

A line of vacation homes clung to the edges of the cliff above her, their vacant windows reflecting the sunlight and without any sign of movement within. The sun seemed out of place in relation to the sea, off to the left from where she would have expected it to be. The wind ripped the surface of the water. She walked on, determined to enjoy herself, until the cliff resolved itself into dunes, and then into flat sand. She guessed she had walked about an hour before she came to a small boardwalk, next to the beach, lined with wooden shacks selling beach equipment and other tourist items. It wasn't surprising, after all, that the Muslim hadn't come. There had been a naïve intensity about him that had made her think she could skip all the small talk. She should have known that she'd be too strange for

him, too moody, too blatantly inexperienced with seductive acts for him to mean it when he said he would
meet her here. What did she care? I will have coffee,
she thought. Coffee. A walk on the beach. Never mind
that he didn't come. Coffee will be nice. The ocean is
the same as always. I'll get back to the hotel in time to
check out. I'll go home. I'll find someone else. Everything is fine.

She made her way up to where the sand was dry. Her
progress grew more labored. She found four wooden
steps leading up from the beach. A weathered wooden
sign beckoned her into a little coffee shop, complete
with orange Naugahyde booths and stools along the
counter. Three boys with knitted ski caps pulled far
down over their ears sat at the far end, fiddling with a
boom box. A man wearing a black T-shirt and jeans
was leaning his elbows on the counter. They all looked
up at her as she entered. She looked back, defiantly,
then away, then down at her hands, then back to the
man behind the counter, then at the boys. Boys that
age had a predatory urgency that unsettled and excited
her all at once. She looked at the man behind the
counter and smiled. He was about her age. She felt a
flush of heat, well, why the hell not? The man she had
planned to meet had abandoned her. Her plan was a
shambles. She sat down at the counter on the stool
closest to the door.

"Coffee, please?" she said.

"No coffee," the man said.

"No coffee?"

"Instant decaf. That's it."

"All right."

He straightened himself up slowly from the counter, resting his hands on the small of his back and stretching in a way that stuck his chest out and that seemed unnecessarily sensual to her. Then he turned away, ripped open a package, and poured brown powder into a cup. He filled it with hot water, found a saucer, and set them down on the counter in front of her. Not very carefully. The liquid spilled over into the saucer. His fingernails were bitten, and dirty. As quickly as it had come, her desire left her.

"Coffee please? Coffee please?" the boys at the end of the counter mimicked.

Not making fun of her, she decided, with a rush of relief, but rather of the man. They were looking at him, not her. And yet how painfully exposed she felt. No doubt she had already betrayed herself. She would drink quickly and pay and get out of there. Everything would be fine.

"Sugar or creamer?" the man said.

"No thank you."

She rested her elbows on the counter and drank. The counter was unpleasantly damp. She took her elbows away again.

Music came, sudden, loud and mindlessly thumping. Now they were all staring at her, nodding in time to the music, as if to assure her it was chosen for her benefit. She looked away. She began to relax. She drank. Then the words of the song—what were they?—forced their way into her mind—*does she go down on you does she go down on you does she go down on you does she go down on you*—

She looked up again to see the man was standing there stupidly, his brows arched into a lewd, wordless question. The boys were laughing and sputtering, looking at her only through the edges of their eyes as they leaned on one another. A weight pressed down on her. She needed to exert conscious effort to expand and contract the muscles of her lungs. She stood up. She would not let them be amused at her expense. She would not.

"I don't care for your music," she said.

Before they could mock her further, she fled out the door and down the four wooden steps to the beach, where she stopped to catch her breath. She thought she might drop there, in the sand, and be sick. She felt a hand on her arm.

"You didn't pay for your coffee," the man said.

"Let go of me, please."

She tried to pull her arm away and found that he gripped her all the more tightly.

"Stop it! Please."

And still he did not let go of her. He smelled of cigarettes. He leered at her. Or was it a leer? Was it in fact a smile? Was this man trying to be seductive, or hostile? She couldn't say. She had no way of telling, these days, what inner motives animated people's outer appearances. Surely his intention was hostile. Surely it was a leer. His face was hideously pockmarked.

"How much do I owe you?" she said.

Heat rose up and made itself known on her face. From desire? No, not from desire, but from shame at ever having felt desire, for this man, even for a moment, and she blushed further knowing that the color in her face would be misinterpreted.

"No charge," the man said. "Come back inside. I told those kids to cut their crap. We have donuts today."

"No. My husband is waiting. I'm sorry. Thank you. I really must go now."

She felt him squeeze her arm. Then he let go. As he released her she felt an odd disappointment. No doubt his intentions had been good. She turned and walked back the way she had come, slowly, head erect, not looking back. She imagined him standing alone on the beach where she had left him, intense and unwavering in his solitude, watching her recede from his view with regret. When she finally turned to see him there, she found that the beach was entirely empty of him, which was not at all what she expected. She began to run, back over the beach, up the long flight of stairs, breathing heavily, a restless terror animating her limbs. When she looked up to see how far she had left to climb she saw the Muslim descending toward her, and she fell on him as if he were her savior.

8

He didn't recognize her until she was almost upon him. Her face was scooped out and emptied of all reason. Her head was flung back, and her mouth open, as if she had been consumed by fear or lust until nothing remained of her. Out of instinct he held her tightly—she was a woman, he a man—and allowed her to compose herself while buried in the corners of his chest. When she looked up at him again he saw that she had almost succeeded in becoming herself. But paler, like a corpse. He pulled the scarf from her head. Ah. There she was. Her hair flew about in all directions. She stepped back, away from him, out of his arms.

"I've been looking for you," he said.

He had not imagined this kind of meeting, here, on some stairs, neither up nor down. He had not imagined this need to speak with her at all. He had imagined her lying in a bed somewhere, naked, silent, open, uncomplicated yet full of mystery, waiting for him, beyond the need for conversation or explanation. But now he would need to suggest something, some interlude, some elaborate seduction, a wasted effort when the outcome was already decided. Hadn't they agreed to meet at a hotel? Wasn't it obvious now what was required of each? And yet to invite her seemed suddenly too crude, and demeaning to them both.

"Hello," she said.

"I'm late," he said. "I'm sorry."

"I wasn't sure you would come."

"Of course I came."

They stood on the stairs, her hair whipping around her face. She no longer looked as if she were going to cry.

"It's very cold," she said.

"Why don't we go inside?"

Wasn't it what she wanted him to say? Wasn't she giving him a reason to invite her back to her room? He felt miserable. Things were not going well.

"There is a sunporch," he said. "I noticed it on the way across the lawn. We could sit there, out of the wind."

She nodded.

They made their way up the stairs, not touching, not any part of them touching, and back across the ragged lawn. She walked in front of him. He was struck by the thinness of her shoulders. He had remembered a

woman more robust than this one. She did not look back
to see if he followed her. He looked up at the hotel as
they approached, and saw a lone guest, an elderly man,
wearing a T-shirt and pajama pants, resting his elbows
on the rail of a second-floor balcony. The man held a
newspaper loosely in one hand. It flapped in the wind.
The man took no notice of them and stared out over
their heads, searching for the horizon, lost in thought,
his lower lip glinting.

They came to a porch enclosed by glass where they
sat down on a wicker sofa facing the sea. They looked
out. The glass was dirty. In places it was difficult to see
through. Her presence overwhelmed him. Her hair was
black and long, with strands of early gray here and there.
Her skin was delicately lined around the eyes; her skin
so pale that he thought he could just discern a ghostly
vein floating underneath her cheek. He felt the sudden
urge to plant small bites along her neck, to leave a trail
of black and blue marks along her white, white skin. He
wanted to grab her by her hair and expose her neck and
feel her yield to him. To feel her knees buckle weakly
and her legs to open to him as he entered her. He ad-
justed the cuffs of his trousers. He cleared his throat.

"I want to explain why I was late," he said.

"It doesn't matter."

"No, I want to," he said. "It's because I forget about
things. Not about you. I've been thinking about you
constantly. But I keep going on like nothing is different. Do you find yourself simply going on? Forgetting
for whole moments things you know you shouldn't?"

She looked at him.

"No," he said. "It's difficult to explain. Sometimes it's as if I could close a book on things I don't want to worry about. I should have filled my car when I had the chance. Instead I ended up driving around a field after an old man on a tractor, asking if he had any fuel to sell. Charged me bootleg rates. You see, I really did want to be here."

He had wanted to conjure up for her an image of himself, ridiculous, driving recklessly over washboarded dirt roads after a friendly old-timer who still insisted on tending to his own crops, even in these times. He left out the details. Just a story. He thought the story would help. To break the ice.

Just past the waves an enormous bird dove for a fish. The beauty of the moment startled him. The singularity of the bird's dive, directly into the small patch of ocean where he happened to be looking at the time, felt like a sign that all would be well, and filled him with grateful exuberance. He felt simple again.

"Will you look at that," he said.

"Do you think it's even possible anymore, what we're doing here," she said. "Everything is so changed. We're living in such a dark time. We don't know what to think about the future. Such an effort to get even this far. You need to ride around after a tractor. It's too much. Do you even desire me?"

"Of course I desire you," he said. But his voice sounded faded and cracked to him, like old paint.

"Why do they keep doing these things to us?" she said. "Why do they hate us so much?"

"I don't know."

Of course he knew generally of what she spoke. He could gauge people's feelings about him these days solely by noting on which side of the great divide they placed him when they asked this same question. Her use of *they* heartened him; it put him firmly in the camp of *us*. His life and happiness had been reduced to a choice of pronouns. He had given up trying to explain the finer subtleties of his beliefs to the people who asked such questions. He made his way through each day shrouded in a sense of profound apology, careful with his words and deeds. And yet he wasn't completely sure of the context of her remark. Everything about her seemed simultaneously remote and intimate. At the moment she did not seem particularly aware of his presence.

"Sometimes I envy them," she said. "I mean, to feel something that deeply. To be that sure of something. I think they are alive in the most pure sense of the word. I think they must feel so much more deeply than ordinary people. They're almost not human anymore. They can look into the eyes of innocents and not be moved. Not reveal their intentions. I try to understand it sometimes. What extraordinary depth of feeling they must have. I would like to feel things so deeply."

"It's a crazy world, all right," he said.

"Everything is so out of balance."

"I don't know."

"I wasn't sure you would come."

He sat next to her and felt the awkwardness between them feed on itself. He wondered whether she would now reveal to him what he knew already about her.

"What do we do now?" she said.

"I suppose this is the reason this sort of thing usually happens at night," he said. "When one is drunk, or tired, and therefore one's inhibitions are weaker."

It wasn't what he meant to say. He didn't even drink alcohol. She was confusing him with her fervent melancholy. He had wanted to tell her the myriad ways he had imagined her. Standing up, naked, arched against a wall, urging him to enter her. On her back in the sand, surf crashing all about. Crouched over him. He felt himself flowing toward her like water toward a depression. Even now in her despair she filled him with a desperate urge to touch her. It could be that she was to be the great passion of his life. He felt that she needed him as well. She was alone in the world. It had been many years since he had been with a new woman. There was no other thing, not his wife, not his children, not even the air, that had sustained him as she had, from the moment he had seen her.

But he said none of those things. Instead he reached over and caressed the back of her neck, under her hair. He felt absurdly bold. She turned to look at him. Her look was boundless and empty, like deep night.

He took his hand away.

She stood up abruptly, as if some internal debate had been decided in favor of standing, and held out her hand.

"It's all right," she said. "Come on, then."

He followed her through the doors of the sunporch to the lobby, down empty hallways, empty of people, empty of voices, empty even of their own voices, to the door that her key unlocked. Someone had left a newspaper on the rug outside her doorway. She picked it up.

"Bombings Will Ravage Economy, Fed Chief Says," she said.

"Ah. Don't read that."

"You know, I am not quite myself today," she said.

"I know."

He took the paper from her and tried to kiss her. She turned away from him, unlocked the door, and walked inside. He took it as a sign to follow that she left the door open behind her. The room was made up perfectly.

"A person could die from such oppressive neatness," she said, and forced a laugh.

She threw back the bedcovers. The scent of bleach wafted up and filled the room with antiseptic sweetness. She sat down on the bed and looked at him strangely. Then she covered her face with her hands. When she looked up again her face was wrinkled, bitter, and arthritic.

"I disgust myself," she said.

He looked at her.

"I don't think I can do this. I'm sorry."

She looked away, at the wall.

He could think of nothing to say.

He walked to the curtain and lifted it.

Not a sea view, as he was hoping, but rather a concrete courtyard with a pool, waterless, kidney-shaped, and cracked. Plastic chaise longues were scattered about, some alone, some circled together, ghostly impressions of some social gathering that had happened once, long ago, or maybe last summer, before the pool was drained, before. Women had lounged in those seats, chatting, keeping one eye on their children splashing in the pool. Rubbing oil on their legs. Pulling the straps of their bathing suits down as far as they could, and telling themselves it was to avoid a tan line, but really it was all about exposing themselves a bit more. Flirting with the lifeguards. Of course something like this would have to happen, he thought. When he had seen her at the trade show she had begun to seduce him almost before they were through with introductions. That never happened to him. Not even when he was young. No wonder she had changed her mind, now that it wasn't late at night, now that she was faced with the reality of him. There was a softness about him lately, his wife often remarked, that made him too amiable to be overtly desirable. He had put on weight. His nose was big. No doubt her curiosity about him had been replaced by active hostility, now that he was here in the flesh and daylight. He wished to be the kind of man who could overpower her objections, to make her want him. But he was not. He should have known better than to think such an interlude would be possible for a man like him, with a woman like her.

Noise came from somewhere outside their door, a muffled cry, the sound of heavy footsteps running past, three or four men, he supposed; then more shouts from the direction of the window, but further away, receding.

He registered these sounds, and let them go again.

"I only want what you want," he said, resigned,

happy even. A weight lifted from his shoulders and he accepted his disappointment as only inevitable. "There is no reason to feel disgusted with yourself."

To his wonder he saw the tension lift from her face, until she looked sixteen, or thirty, and he knew that she had somehow chosen him after all.

"All right," she said. "It's what we came for. But I need you to go away again for a few minutes. I'm sorry. I want to get ready. Just a few minutes. Fifteen minutes. Take the key, let yourself in again. Don't knock. Fifteen minutes."

He nodded. She handed him the key somehow without quite touching his hand, without quite looking at him. That was all right. He went to the door, opened it, and heard it latch behind him.

And so he found himself outside, in the hallway, separated by a door from the woman who would soon be his lover after all. Maybe. It was difficult to say. A tension rose up in him, making him pace back and forth along the long and silent hallways. Again he felt the phantom thrill, the fleeting terror. Something was going to happen here. Something he didn't understand. We are poised on the edge, he thought. A moment like this comes just before taking vows. Just before dying. Committed, but not yet set in motion.

9

She got up from the bed and went to a suitcase. She threw it on the bed, opening it, digging through it for what she needed, full of purpose, or past caring, she didn't know which, but she did know what she wanted, she had probably known all along what she wanted, at least for now. She found what she barely remembered packing. She dressed deliberately, with care, just as she had many hundreds of times before. She put on stockings and pumps, her slip, her silk blouse, her good navy suit. All as it had been, the last time she was with her husband. She zipped the suitcase closed and dragged it onto the floor. She made the bed up again, tucking in the sheets, arranging the pillows, and lay down on top of the bedcover, on her side, facing away from the door, using her hand as a pillow, just like before, and waited. Perhaps she willed herself to sleep. She heard the door open and felt his presence in the room again. She felt him standing by the edge of the bed. She kept her eyes closed, her breathing relaxed.

"What do you want me to do?" he said.

"Take my clothes off," she said. Irritated that she needed to explain. "Leave yours on. Then lie down next to me."

The bed creaked when he put his weight on it. She felt him lie behind her, and his arms encircled her fully clothed waist, and for a moment her desire left her, to be replaced with something equally rich and complicated, but softer, almost maternal. Then he began to undress her and the maternal feeling fled, and instead she saw the hideously pockmarked face, the nicotine-stained, nail-bitten fingers. She saw boys in knitted ski caps chanting in the background about coffee and pussy. She saw thick fingers on the back of her neck. She saw her brother-in-law. She saw grocery boys. She saw debasement and terror and chaos. Infection. He would infect her. What is this? What is this? He had gone too far, he wasn't meant to go this far, her husband hadn't gone this far. A crumbling, inward, the veil was ripped away, the membrane collapsed. She was dying now. She dove more deeply inside herself and touched the idea of violence, lightly, in her mind, and saw how attractive violence was to her, how she longed to be above this man, to have him crouched below, compliant, barely murmuring. Colors flashed across her inner lid, purple, green, yellow. Then came a stark, surprising perception of the body itself; this, this wetness, this messiness, there was no other word for it, he had removed her hose and panties and bra and she was splayed across the bed in a most unseemly fashion; she became aware of how her limbs were arranged; awareness flooded over her like a rush of air after swimming to the surface. She kept very still, she moved not at all, until the last breath, when she planned to run away to some far corner of her mind. He will come into an empty room, she thought, but no, he was in there, with her, pulling her back, pulling her back, he would not leave without her, until there was no help for it, until she had to wrench free of him—get off, get off!—rather than be betrayed by her own body.

And there he was, this stranger, quiet now, kissing her between her legs. She was dazzled by her lack of understanding of it all. She thought she might be sick. I want to be sad, she thought. I should be sad. These love acts should mean nothing more to me than memories of the grave. I will not be moved. I will not be confused. I will be calm. I must never be moved again. If I am moved again I will forget my husband, which I must never do.

He looked up at her. And those other thoughts left her, until all she could feel was a polite indifference, and there she was, and he was just a man, he was just this man, who was for some reason now looking at her with what resembled loving tenderness.

When exactly fifteen minutes had passed he unlocked the door. The room was dark. She was lying on her side, away from him, wearing what looked to be a woman's suit. Navy. With shoes to match. It was not what he expected.

"What do you want me to do?" he said.

"Take my clothes off," she said. "Leave yours on. Then lie down next to me."

He came to her, lying next to her bed and encircling her waist with his arm, and as he did so he recognized the scene for what it was. Something deeply intimate.

More than casual lovers. It was familiar to him. He knew what to do.

"Tell me if I get it wrong," he whispered.

He pulled himself closer to her, breathing in the scent of her hair. She gave no reaction. She could have been asleep for all the attention she paid to him. But she was not asleep. He knew that. No. She was merely passive, giving him permission to do with her what he would. Her passivity filled him with nearly unbearable desire to violate her. He removed her suit jacket with clumsy difficulty. Her arms flopped out of their sleeves. He reached around and began to unbutton the blouse, less careful now, more impatient, until he was ready to pull it off as well and see his first glimpse of her bare stomach, her bra. Her arms became entangled in the sleeves of the blouse; he had forgotten to undo the buttons at the cuffs. The blouse twisted about her wrists. She made a small sound. He lifted her skirt and reached roughly inside her underpants, and she made the sound again, a whimper, a barely audible protest, but offered no physical resistance, only a languid heaviness that responded to the slightest force by rearranging her limbs to ease his way until his fingers were inside her and he was feeling all of her. His fingers found the rim of her diaphragm. Yes, that's right, he thought. Whatever game we are playing here, this belongs, it belongs, like everything else here belongs, to the language of committed lovers. It occurred to him that he was playing the role of a dead man. The thought fell over him as if he had discovered the truth of a great mystery and he wanted to weep. He felt her squeeze his fingers and a flood of passion drowned out his reason. He took his hand out from inside of her and yanked at her hose and pants and threw them down, no longer slow and patient, no longer taking care, no longer caring. He managed to pull the blouse from where it had wrapped itself about her wrists. He unhooked her bra and kneaded her breasts, then pulled away her skirt, until she was white and naked and he was still fully clothed and her eyes were still closed tightly, as if feigning sleep, except for the pulsing tension in her jaw. She lay limp before him, splayed. He was filled with her animal smell, loamy, with the hint of decay. She was so very naked now, so absolutely naked and exposed, lying on her back, her eyes closed, her body filled with the same torpor as before, the same looseness of limbs, as if to signal to him that she was entirely at his disposal. He lifted her head roughly by the hair as he straddled her, willing her to open her eyes; then let her go, and her head flopped back down on the bed, and still no reaction came from her. He kissed her deeply. When he was done she lay with her mouth wide open and slack, and her eyes were still closed, her breathing at war with itself. Did she want to fellate him? Did she expect it? Her body was flush with arousal, but she did not touch herself. Her mouth was so very open. Her breathing came in shallow gasps, as if from grief or hysteria. Aroused and confused, afraid of his own urges, he turned her over abruptly on the bed so he didn't need to look at that face. Now that he could not see her closed eyes he felt more in control, and without ceremony, he unzipped himself and grabbed his cock and took her from behind, he, still fully clothed; she, naked, and facing away, and remote, just as all women are remote in this particular act of love-making; except this time something different happened, because when he felt her squeezing him, and began to feel his own release pouring into her, she turned to look at him with a look of, not rapture, oh no! but something very close to disgust. Get off, get off! she might have said, between clenched teeth, barely audible, and jerked her hips away to spill him out of her before either of them climaxed, and there he was, dribbling out all over her buttocks and thighs. He knelt in front of her, horrified, seeking exoneration, sure that she could not forgive him for being so rough, feeling that he might perhaps cry in his frustration and embarrassment, and kissed her over and over again between her open legs. She touched his head, then ran her fingers through his hair, as if she were searching diligently for something she had lost.

I'm sorry," she said.

"Oh no. It is I who should be sorry."

"Oh, let's not be sorry," she said. "We have time to try again. It's been so very long for me. Ages and ages. You wouldn't believe how long it has been for me."

She lay without covering herself, embarrassing him. Her words gave him a significance that he wasn't sure how to interpret. Flustered, he searched for any words to relieve his discomfort.

"How completely naked you are," he said.

She laughed.

"Not like you," she said.

It seemed as if she were blaming him for that, and all at once his clothes oppressed him, and he felt ashamed once more of his lack of finesse, of the way he had bungled it. It occurred to him that he would perhaps feel less overwhelmed by her nakedness if he also took his clothes off. So he undressed, awkwardly, not looking at her. He took care to take his socks off before his trousers, because just then it seemed to him that there could be no greater embarrassment than to have a woman see him with his socks on and no trousers. He folded his clothes neatly on a chair, aware that her gaze was fixed on him, and joined her on the bed, not touching her, feeling frightfully bulky and unattractive compared with her. He leaned back on the pillow as if at ease and rested his arms behind his head, to minimize his paunch, and looked at her, and tried to think of something to say or do. There was something so American about her build, so muscular. It shocked him to realize he was sitting here with her and thinking about his wife's breasts, earthy and pendulous. He put his wife out of mind. The widow was looking at him rather pointedly. His privates were all right. There was nothing particularly outstanding about them, but nothing to be ashamed of, either. She looked at him with an odd detachment. As if they had not made love at all.

"I didn't expect that you would be circumcised," she said.

A churning motion began inside his mind. The comment seemed excessively personal, and excessively ignorant, and not entirely complimentary, and yet she sounded disappointed.

"It's customary," he said.

"I really know nothing about you at all," she said.

He wondered whether she was referring to him as an individual or as a member of a larger community of men whom she had assumed to be uncircumcised. He decided, abruptly, to forgive her. They hadn't had time for getting to know one another in any other way except one. He remembered the feeling of her muscle squeezing him; the slope of her neck as she leaned against him.

"You know a great deal," he said. "You know everything you need to know. I'm a simple man."

He stroked her hair.

"And you?" he said. "Who are you?"

"Oh, nothing," she said.

"That must get confusing," he said.

He waited for her to continue. Why did she not speak of what he knew already to be true? He touched her arm and tried to be patient. He imagined that her thoughts must now be of her late husband. His mind skittered across memories of its own. He felt his eyes dart about the room almost independently of him, to the lamp, the television set on its stand, the ceiling, finding rest in hers.

"You're a very beautiful woman," he said.

"Do you really think so?"

"You know it without me telling you."

"I don't know anything."

"In that case, you are ugly. I'm the only man who will ever want you. You might as well stay with me."

"I might."

A shadow fell over her face. He did not want to ask her the reason. He wanted her to volunteer it, just as she had volunteered her body to him. Although they were lying naked together, exchanging what passed for intimacies, he hesitated to breach her privacy. He would have liked to ask her what she was feeling, but he was afraid of sounding falsely sympathetic. He wanted also to ask her why she had pushed him away at the very moment when he felt her coming closer. But he was momentarily caught up with a strange fantasy, that too many words would get in the way of complete understanding, an understanding beyond words, the result of their lovemaking and the tragedy they had both known in their lives. It was the kind of understanding he had imagined marriage would bring him, yet understanding his wife's inner thoughts had eluded him. His wife had become ever more inscrutable across the years and throughout their shared experiences, hiding behind her correct behavior, wearing her principles like clothing, and therefore never completely naked with him. Or worse, the thought struck him, it could be that there were no deeper layers of woman behind the façade. He was married to an empty dress, as shallow as the cotton.

"Isn't what we're doing a sin in your religion?" the widow said.

"There's a story," he said. "A sinner came to the Prophet to confess the crime of sleeping with a woman. The Prophet said, 'Allah has concealed your sin, and so should you.'"

"I think that story means you can do whatever you like as long as nobody finds out."

"Not exactly. But I like your interpretation."

She rolled away from him onto her back, her legs parted in a casual way that delighted him. And yet she had traveled away from him again; she was being free only because she had forgotten about him. Her nipples were a wonder to him, soft, pink, almost transparent, like the inside of a conch shell.

"Look, I know who you are," he said abruptly.

He watched her change, a confusion of emotions crossing over her features until she finally forced them back into a blank indifference.

"You know nothing," she said.

"I know you," he said. "I know everything about you. I didn't know when I met you, but I discovered it later."

"You don't know anything."

"I saw the pictures. A picture of you making a speech. You were shaking hands with the governor."

"You didn't see anything."

"I did research. You were on the front page of the *Los Angeles Times* last winter. Anyone can see it. I don't know why you weren't more honest with me."

She looked at him steadily, her eyes flat and defeated. He wished that he had said nothing at all.

"I can't tell you how terrible it all is," she whispered.

He wasn't sure whether she referred to him, or the fate of her husband, or the general state of the world.

"It must have been very hard for you," he said. "I'm sorry."

"Oh, I don't know," she said, suddenly relaxed again, looking away from him and almost smiling, almost looking like that woman he had seen in the magazines: stoic, undefeated.

"Oh, I don't know," she said again, and sighed. "I started taking Zoloft. I put on a lot of weight, it made me fat, but God, I survived."

She sounded as if she had said it before, many times. Perhaps to a talk show host. Her eyes squeezed shut, then flashed open again on him.

"You must think I'm crazy," she said. "So why did you come?"

He hesitated, considering the ways he could reply to her question. How to explain how her invitation had touched him? How to make clear the void in which he found himself these days, a place from which almost all touching had ceased, even the most casual gesture of warmth taken away, erased by his birthright? His wife was oblivious to such snubs. This woman, he felt certain, would understand. He could walk through crowds and feel the bodies shy away from him. He was followed about by the eyes of strangers, everywhere, mothers, children, soldiers, police officers, oh yes, the eyes watched him, looking for some sign of his evildoing, he could have been a leper the way those eyes looked at him! How biblical were his sufferings! He recognized it as a Western reaction to his situation. And why not? He had lived here more than half his lifetime. That she, of all people, would want to touch him! She of all people!

"I came because you asked me," he said.

"Do you do anything a strange woman asks you?"

No, no, he had never done such a thing before.

"Sometimes," he said.

"Is there no other reason? Morbid curiosity? Something like that?"

"No! Of course not. A little. Really, it's simple. You're a very beautiful woman. At my age a man begins to wonder."

"Curiosity," she said. "Vulgar, morbid curiosity."

"No."

He leaned over to touch her breast, and when she pushed his hand away he patted her hair, wanting somehow to arrange it as well as her feelings into something more loving, less angry. He felt himself brushed with the darkness of her grief, which seemed to curl into his mouth like old smoke that he wanted to expel.

"Look, I want to get to know you," he said. "I want to understand you. I think two people can learn to understand one another, even as different as we are, even if all we have together is just one night."

"You want to understand me," she said.

"Yes, yes, to understand you," he said. "I want that. This sort of thing is all very unusual to me. I'm sorry if I say the wrong thing."

She said nothing.

"And you?" he said. "Why did you invite me? A strange choice. Wouldn't you say that it's a very strange choice?"

"Yes. Very strange."

"I wonder."

He resolved to push his sense of awkwardness away and to take control of the situation, to act like a man.

He leaned over her and took her face firmly in his two hands, and kissed it, over and over again, first gently and then with increasing force, but not on the mouth, never on the mouth, because she kept turning away from him, until she pushed him away entirely and stood up, taking the sheet with her to cover her nakedness, and walked to the window and opened it, leaving only the curtain between them and the outside world, a gauze curtain billowing in a wind that invaded the room. She looked out, as if searching for the view he knew wasn't there. The light was slanted now.

"Tell me about your wife," she said.

"I love her."

"Do you?"

"Of course. We are very happy together. We have two daughters. They are good girls. They are on the honor roll."

"Then why did you come?"

Why did she insist? He looked at her, standing alone by the window with a sheet clutched to her chest. Her face was so open now, so stark, that he felt momentarily off-balance, as if he were falling into it. He wondered if it was the nature of her attraction: her stark emotionality, her willingness to feel. So unlike his wife.

"I came because of you," he said.

"I wonder if you love your wife as much as I loved my husband."

"I don't know."

"I loved him very much, you know. But he's gone, and now that I'm with you I can barely remember him."

"Isn't that a good thing?" he ventured. "To move on?"

"No, that is not a good thing," she said. "It is a bad thing. A wicked thing. And pointless. It's remarkable how pointless making love can be."

He did not take her remark personally. He was too filled up with the reality of her, naked, with only a sheet between them and their next lovemaking; he barely heard the words she spoke. He had been inside her already once, and would soon be again. He understood that now, that all these words and gestures were a kind of game, one that would not affect the eventual outcome. She was very beautiful to him, standing there by the window. He imagined her ravaged by the realization that her husband was gone forever. He had a fleeting vision of her doing harm to herself, stepping out into traffic perhaps, to get away from the pain. He saw himself there with her, as if the two of them were simultaneously in two places, one where she stood at the window, alone, and another, equally real, where he was cradling her in his arms and covering her with his tears and caresses. It saddened him to think of her in pain like that. It reflected in her face. She had an intensity. A capacity for suffering.

He sat up on the edge of the bed. He tried to look worldly, sitting there, naked, as if he were used to that sort of thing.

"Look, we're talking too much," he said. "Come here."

She surprised him by not arguing. Instead she closed

the window neatly, then came over to the bed and lay
down, spreading herself out like a bower, like a sacrifice, her arms languid and weightless above her head,
her legs curved demurely together and away from him.
Her face had closed up again into something super-
ficial and bland. She looked at the wall. He wanted to
make it up to her, to make up for all the impatience and
clumsiness of their first sex. He was not so interested
this time in fulfilling his own impulses. For the moment he felt sated. But he wanted to be with her, to be
gentle with her, to make her feel safe enough that she
would risk exposing her passions to him. He traced the
curve from her chin to her neck, then ran his fingertips
over her collarbone. He wanted to explore and cata-
logue her textures and valleys. He felt more cartogra-
pher than lover. She said nothing. Nor did she look at
him. Her continued sexual passivity puzzled and mad-
dened him. It's possible that she was feeling violated
by his ministrations. Or bored. He couldn't say. But
at least she did not ask him to stop. He ran his palms
along the inside of her legs and across her mons, rubbing each breast in tender, patient circles. Patient. Above
all he wanted to be patient. She was still recovering
from her loss, obviously. It had fallen upon him to heal
her. It impressed him that she could be so completely
disinterested in making him feel good about his meth-
ods. Her body was slack and unresponsive. He opened
her legs and began to kiss her thighs. She made no sign.
Encountering no resistance, he pushed his face into her
pubis and licked her. Her taste was shockingly unpleas-

ant. She tasted of aluminum and iron filings and anti-
bacterial agents. He wanted to excuse himself, to beg
pardon, to beg off.

"Oh, don't do that," she said, slapping ineffectually
at the top of his head. "Oh, please don't do that. I just
am never comfortable with that sort of thing. Oh, I
don't know. You can't like doing that. Please."

Her protestations fortified him. He pressed on. He
licked slowly, pushing himself past his discomfort at
her medicinal taste, until she lay there, absolutely still,
engorged and glistening and nonetheless unrelentingly
distant. He licked. He could have been water dripping
on a glacier. And yet he took hope in signs of a thaw.
Her unpleasant flavor was gradually being transposed
to an elusive but unmistakable taste of arousal. The
muscles in a thigh resting against his cheek fluttered
and twitched. She may have moaned. A gamy scent
rose up from her. She was close, close. Then she inexplicably faded away from him again until she lay flat
and dull under his tongue.

Never mind. He moved his tongue again, slowly,
gently, not insisting on anything from her. Nothing at
all. He persisted. A stiffness grew between his shoulder
blades. He ignored it, feeling that she must be coming
closer to some release. He was patient. He led her up
that same slow river again and felt the twitches and
moans once more from her, which again fell away; and
he once more felt nothing from her, not even frustration. He persevered. The nub of her eluded him, bur-
rowing away whenever he drew too near. He began to
doubt. His tongue felt cauterized, numbed by the sper-

micide. He felt old. He felt unskilled and unmuscular and unschooled in the ways of woman. Where was she now? The body he administered to felt uninhabited. He was alone. He had fallen alone into some restless purgatory, a liquid place as wide as the sea where waves and waves of thwarted desire rose up and threatened to engulf him, but the waves at the last moment would inexplicably dissipate, and he would find himself in waters flat and unmoving, where he was becalmed, where all desire left him. He discovered himself to be exhausted. A dullness filled his mouth and greater dullness filled his mind. His jaw ached. The pain between his shoulder blades grew more insistent. He was afraid to move, to adjust his position, since this woman would surely take it as a sign of his impatience and then whatever gains he might have made would be lost. In frustration he pressed his face more deeply into her folds until he found what he was looking for, and rubbed her hard across his lips, his teeth. She whimpered, hardly a sound at all, and he felt her knees drawing together to protect herself.

He stopped.

"Did I hurt you?" he said.

"Oh no. You have given me the most wonderful sensations," she said. "Thank you."

She lay there, thanking him, until he was completely certain that she had felt nothing. He ran a hand from knee to thigh to pubis, expecting to hear himself murmur something reassuring, and found instead that he was grabbing her, angry, at the crotch. Her body grew rigid. He saw her clench her teeth and look away, nei-

ther protesting nor acceding to him, which enraged
him further—why had she come here if not to enjoy
herself?—and he leaned over, close to a breast, which
seemed to him just then to be childlike and vulnerable
and therefore the perfect place to breach her defenses.
He felt his mouth close over and bite, hard, on the nip-
ple. She clutched his head closer to her, in response to
the pain, letting out an earthy rumble and swiveling
her hips toward him until there was no help for it, and
he hammered at her until she was nothing more than a
banner snapping in the wind.

12

If I think of my husband, this man
will have no hold on me, she thought, and with that
thought to brace her, she joined him on the bed again.
She lay back and closed her eyes. She understood, in-
tellectually at least, this man's wish to please her, to
give her a gift in the form of sexual generosity. Her husband had not been one to make such gestures. His sexual generosity was of a more conventional sort. He had
taken great pride in his ability to maintain control of
his climax, a control that had allowed him to pound her
for an hour at a time or more, without any yielding, or
loss of discipline, or weakening of his erection. He

used to drop out of bed in the morning to the floor and do thirty push-ups, a ritual he repeated at night and two other times during the course of the day, and he used those same muscles to plow her, diligently, all the while politely holding his weight off of her, until all desire left her, until she was used up, weak, and boneless. Her husband had disliked sexual kissing. He felt it to be both unsanitary and messy. He refused to come in her mouth. He had gainfully tried giving her oral pleasure once and so clearly disliked it, as much as he had tried to hide it from her, that she told him that she derived no pleasant feelings from it, and was happy to forgo that particular pleasure since it gave him none. They always used a condom as well as a diaphragm. Their sex was neat. They had married young. She was never unfaithful to him, not physically at any rate; nor did she resent his way of showing affection. His way of loving her was too wrapped up in his sense of self, in his disciplined nature, for him to change.

Once when she had been stricken with a great flu, the kind that had left her wrung out with fever and continuously retching until her eyes were bloodshot and her gums swollen, her husband had nursed her around the clock, feeding her tiny shavings of ice, making sure she drank enough water, half carrying her to the bathroom on the hour to give her a chance to urinate; giving her frequent sponge baths to keep her spirits up. It had done her good whenever she rose up out of her fever and opened her eyes to see him there, ready to leap to her aid. It was a level of devotion that astounded her and that she had never been able to reciprocate completely. It was a standing joke between them that her way of doctoring was to leave him to get well. On the worst day of her illness when even the bed-sheet next to her skin had pained her, he had found a way to massage her feet that had caused her no dis-comfort, and he rubbed her feet in that same gentle manner until her body radiated with relaxed well-being, and she slept. "I should bottle that remedy," he would joke for years after.

Now she was being touched by a far more liquid sort of man. His touch was almost feminine. The bound-aries were uncertain. She was not sure of her role. This man used his tongue a great deal. She was shamed by the realization that she was a sexual naïf, even at her age. Even with all her preparations and planning she had never once imagined the wet reality of him inside of her, of his cock resting against her insides without a rubber between them. Her imagination had never taken her to that moment, but instead had left her at the threshold of something vague and sexless. The reality of him this close to her center filled her with confusion and a sense of shame. Not only for what he was doing but for what he was. She was momentarily horrified to imagine what deep motivation had caused her to seek him out, a motivation driven not by her conscious will but by some other force, as if she were possessed by demons. She tried to relax and think of other things. His approach was so alien to her experience that it aroused curiosity in her rather than desire. He didn't seem to mind. If anything, he slowed down. For a while she forgot about him. There was so much else to think about. About his question, for example. What were her motives for inviting him? What were they? He continued to distract her with his touchings until she felt only irritation at him, wanting him to stop, and not wanting him to, because if he stopped he would want to speak again and just now she wanted to think.

And then he bit her. A cacophonous roar rose up from her belly to her throat. It shocked her to realize that the sound she heard coming out of her mouth resembled not a cry of protest; rather, it was nothing other than a deep purr. She clutched him to her and bit back, on the shoulder, and felt him grab her around the throat as he entered her and shake her back and forth over himself, over and over again, until she could do nothing but say yes. Her hips bucked and lunged around him quite independently of her mind until she felt the harpy rise up in her and ride, laughing and screaming, and her body betrayed her and found its own release. Now he was lying on top of her. She may have heard sobbing. He stayed inside of her. Although he was heavy for her, and his skin damp, she did not push him away. She felt her body gripping at him, over and over again, trying to hold on as he receded from her, until he finally slipped out, and they were apart. He fell off of her and they lay side by side and she felt once more the grief of being alone.

I must love him, she thought. I must love him, to allow him here inside of me this way, to allow him to move me so. She felt exhausted, defeated.

"What are you thinking?" he said.

"I was thinking," she murmured, at the edge of

sleep, "I was thinking about you. You're my first, you know."

"Your first?"

"First Muslim," she said. "First Arab."

"But I am not an Arab," he said. "I am Persian. There are great historical differences. And I am not particularly religious. Really, I'm the most secular sort of Muslim you're ever going to meet."

But she was already asleep.

13

should leave now, he thought. I should never have come. She is wrapped up in an abnormal grief, an erotic fantasy that I want no part of. And the sex is not so good.

He did not, after all, leap up immediately. He tried to understand himself. The woman's body next to him was efficient rather than erotic. Her labia were meager, like retread on an old tire. There was nothing generous about her body. She was evidently preoccupied with some morbid need that he barely understood. He should never have come.

She was lying on her side as she slept, facing him,

with the sheet covering her, accentuating the hill of her hips. He ought to go, he told himself, he ought to go; and yet he found himself unable to restrain himself from lifting the sheet so that he could see her naked again, especially now that her body was sprawled out in deep slumber and defenseless before his examination. The patch of fur between her legs and the gentle dark of her nipples filled him with a giddy longing, but he did not touch her or himself to relieve it. He looked at her body for long minutes, taking guilty pleasure in his role of voyeur, torturing himself with the thought that surely one kiss on the soft curve of her stomach wouldn't awaken her. But he didn't touch her. Proud of his self-control, he stood up at last, found his clothes, and dressed. He would leave her there to sort out her own problems. His legs and shoulders were trembling with sharp aftershocks from their last lovemaking. He hoped he hadn't bruised her. He had no desire to be cruel. She had suffered enough, poor woman. He dressed deliberately, needing to think over each movement as if he were performing a task unfamiliar to his hands and feet. By the time he had stepped into his trousers and succeeded in buttoning his shirt his thinking had modified itself somewhat. There was no need for hasty decision making. Instead of leaving immediately he would take a brief walk, to clear his head and to stretch his limbs, and to give her time to sleep. He could also get some things from his car, if he decided in the end to stay. He picked up the key from where she had left it on the bedside table. Take the key, and then I can come back again without needing to knock and awaken her, he thought. I don't have to decide anything now. I can leave the key at the desk if I decide to go now.

He opened the door and closed it behind him.

The hallway runner, faded and threadbare in places, stretched out in both directions in a numbing pattern of diamonds and crosses. Between every two doors along the walls was a fleur-de-lis sconce. The lighting was dim. Some of the lamps were burned out. He walked softly along empty hallways to the lobby, where he was grateful to see a man sitting behind the front desk. The man gave him a half wave and smiled. He waved in return, happy for the contact. Otherwise the lobby was deserted, and dark at the corners, as if the management had decided to conserve by buying lights of insufficient wattage.

He decided to take a stroll, both to stretch his legs and to clear his head. He turned to go out the back of the hotel, toward the ocean, and was surprised to see through the back windows that the sunlight lived still, through all that had happened to him since he had last thought of the sun. He made his way through the porch where they had first sat, through its glass doors, over the lawn and to the edge of the cliff overlooking the water. The wind from that afternoon had died down almost completely. The sky was overcast. A blood-red groove separated the sky and the sea, both of which lay stippled and flat and gray. Then the sun dipped below the horizon and all went dark without a hint of transition from day to night. He stood completely still and willed himself to comprehend the beauty of the moment, but all he could think was that he had seen it all before. He stood there for several minutes, trying to feel appropriately moved, long enough to feel the damp air settle on his skin. Now that it was dark he felt reluctant to climb down the staircase to the beach and walk along it as he had planned. He could just see a ragged line of white when a wave broke; otherwise the scene below him was a void of fog and gray where any sort of person might be lurking and watching him. The sound of the surf steadied him. What to do now? The prudent thing would be to go away from here. Send her the money later, if necessary, for the room. But that wouldn't do at all. If he drove home now he would arrive too early to accommodate the lie he had told his wife, that he was flying to the East Coast for a business meeting and wouldn't be back before the following evening. He would need to rent some other room en route, a room without a naked woman in the bed to warm him. Ridiculous! What a waste of a lie! No. He would stay. Of course he would stay. After he had a chance to recover they would make love again, this time more perfectly and more tenderly than before. He had no other choice. She had come into his life as sudden as a knife edge, dividing him from the monotony of his days. He called up the memory of her naked, sleeping, with her body open in slumber, and his own body reacted with such delight that it drove all other thoughts away that were not of her—her hair, her breasts, her snatch—until he shouted into the void beyond the cliff, and heard the sea roar swallow up the sound of his voice and spit it back at him again.

14

She dreamed she was at a gas station. She needed to urinate. When she opened the door to the rest room she found she had stumbled into what looked to be an airport terminal. A sign above her said EINGANG. A guard asked for her identity papers. She looked down and saw that somehow she had ripped them up; her documents lay in tattered heaps on the floor by her feet. *Sie hat keinen Pass!* the guard shouted, and she found herself surrounded by soldiers who were pointing their guns and shouting orders at her. Before they could arrest her she fled back through the door to the gas station, where she was relieved to see her husband filling their tank. "It's the strangest thing," she told him. "Go through that door over there, and you're in Germany. East Germany, I think." Her husband said, "I'm good at faces, but not so good at names. Won't you tell me yours again?" Horrified, she found that she could not. A paralysis in her mouth prevented her from speaking. "That's all right," her husband said. He narrowed his eyes in a way that was unfamiliar to her. "People like you," he said. "I know what to call you. There is a name for people like you." Then he grabbed her and kissed her in a way he had never kissed her in real life, his tongue in her throat, his rough beard rasping at her lips, waking her up.

The dream filled her with such anxiety and revulsion that she closed her eyes again, trying to discover the source of its power over her. She and her husband had traveled to Germany together early in their marriage, so that part of the dream had some basis in fact. She could remember no unpleasant associations with the trip, however, except for a wistful regret that her husband hadn't chosen Spain or Italy for their first trip to Europe together, rather than a place that had seemed quite cold to her. Why the dream should return her to that place and time baffled her.

She had dreamed of her husband once before, shortly after his death. In that dream her husband had stretched out his arms to her and smiled beatifically, and she awoke with a deep sense of peace, a feeling that wherever he was, he was happy. But in this most recent dream her husband had adopted that stiff-shouldered posture of his, the one that had been his way to signal his disapproval of her. He used to go on for days or weeks, never quite telling her what she had done, and never quite admitting that he was unhappy with her. It unsettled her to have the peaceful feeling from one dream snatched away capriciously by the next. Was nothing at all to be depended on?

She became aware that she was alone in the bed and opened her eyes. Had he left her? Had he gone away for good? She groped for the light and turned it on. No sign of him. He had accomplished what he had set out to do and he had left her. His clothes were missing. And yet the scent of him remained. Everywhere. Inside of her. She felt marked, infected, abused. Nothing was as she had imagined it. He was strange to her. His skin was an unfamiliar color. His penis inside her smaller than her memory of how a penis should feel. He wore cologne. He stood too close. He pronounced his words too carefully. He was one of them. She had chosen him because there was no possibility of loving him. But instead of extinguishing this strange, irrational, unpredictable desire that had risen up in her in recent weeks, he had inflamed it. He had made her body come. She had intended to keep at least that part of her out of this situation, but her body had gone galloping off of its own accord with this satyr, this troll. It could only mean that she harbored feelings for him. She felt her anxiety beginning to mount. She rubbed at her skin, her vulva. Surely her body's release was nothing more than an animal instinct, one that she could reproduce, here, without him or without any thought of tenderness. She rubbed, trying to prove some point that lay forgotten beneath the shifting intentions of her will, intentions that seemed quite out of her control. Then she heard the key in the lock and felt herself fold up, neatly and quickly, until she was civilized again, with only modest moods and lights of face and body.

"I thought I would get my things from the car," he said, and lit a small lamp near the door.

He smiled the smile of an idiot child.

"I thought you would have had enough of me," she said.

"Of course not."

"I'm sorry. Things have been very extreme for me, lately."

"I understand," he said.

He was carrying a shaving kit and small overnight bag.

"You travel light," she said.

"I didn't expect to need much."

He laid his bag down on his side of the bed, kissed her, and went into the bathroom, carrying the shaving kit.

She lay on the bed and listened to the sounds of his toilet. She felt closer to some reality, some truth about who and what she was. Being naked with a strange man had a glittering clarity all its own, stripping away a residue that had clung to her for months now. What had she come for, again? To be close to a man of his kind. Love your enemy. Something like that. She stood up and followed him into the bathroom, not bothering to cover herself. He had taken out his razor and shaving cream and had begun to lather his face.

"I thought I would shave for you," he said. "Unless you like the feeling of your skin being rubbed raw?"

She didn't answer.

"Well, in any case, I'll finish here what I've begun. We'll save that rougher experience for some other time."

His act of shaving had a concreteness to it, a reference to normality that heartened her. It had been so long. But look, the man himself was wrong. Some anxious parody of her husband. Too dark and too short and too broad. Except she could hardly remember having a husband, at this moment, because she was flooded with another image, of black-haired men slowly shaving their arms and legs and chests, gliding the edge of a straight-edged razor over every inch of their skin, with self-referential eroticism and with ritualistic precision, preparing themselves for their coming sacrifice and resurrection.

He smiled at her through the lather.

"We could go out," he said. "Get some food. Unless you'd rather not."

She stood behind him and watched them both in the mirror. She was naked, he fully clothed. Just as before. She watched her arms encircle him from behind.

"That's nice," he said, and leaned into her as he shaved.

She watched herself kiss the back of his neck. His neck was surprisingly warm. She put both hands around it and discovered she could nearly, but not completely, encircle it with her fingers. Then she rested her hands on his shoulders, enjoying the warmth of his skin through his starched cotton shirt. Familiar. Not familiar.

He began to shave his neck.

"You aren't what you seem," he said.

"No," she said. "And you are not what you seem. Where are you from?"

"Originally? Tehran. But long ago. You knew that. You asked me before."

"How long ago did you leave there?"

"Oh, many years."

"Don't you go back?"

"No."

"Why not?"

He had nicked himself by his ear. A spot of red bled through the lather.

"Bad memories," he said.

"Bad memories," she said, and silently approved of the way it sounded, cinematic and uncomplicated.

She dropped her arms and walked back into the bedroom. Her skirt and blouse and hose and underclothes were lying about on the floor where he had thrown them when he had first undressed her. The disorder of her own things oppressed her. She felt the urge to stuff all of her clothes into the trash, to clean up the traces of their behavior. She found herself instead picking up her discarded clothes carefully, one piece at a time, and hanging them up in the closet. Wasn't she just about to throw them away? Her sense of time and volition were exceptionally fluid. She hardly knew what to expect of herself. Was it the scent of their sex that made it so? Yes, the smell in this room ignited a warmth in her that blossomed and spread to her fingertips and radiated outward. She wondered how it would feel to bring her new, radiating self out into the world, on the arm of this exotic man who was now shaving himself for her in the bathroom. Would he take her hand? Would they walk down the street in some more intimate manner, hip to hip, telegraphing their eroticism to all passersby, he touching her on her ass or under her shirt, not caring who saw, even wanting them to see? Later on he would rub her inner thighs and pinch her nipples into an erection in the corner of some darkened restaurant while the bartender looked on.

No. That wasn't right.

Reeling from the cheapness of that image, she abruptly found herself lost in another, of him sitting in her kitchen, in her home. She, frying eggs perhaps. The coffee brewing. Or better yet take him to her mother's, where he would be compliant, respectful; he would use his impeccable manners throughout her mother's elaborate meal. On the menu would be one of her mother's specialties, veal or pork no doubt, finished off with one of her mother's three favorite dessert recipes, prepared only for special guests on special occasions. After dinner he would volunteer to wash the dishes, and she would love him all the more with his black-haired forearms plunging into the suds in her mother's sink, and when the dishes were washed and dried and put away they would keep her mother company by watching *Wheel of Fortune* with her before they retired upstairs to the guest room, a room full of tatting and stuffed chairs and antimacassars, where they would have a sweaty fuck under her mother's hand-crocheted afghans, whispering for the sake of decorum. The next morning she would leave him sleeping in the bed and creep down just after dawn to find her mother already awake, squeezing orange juice in the kitchen, and they would have a mother-daughter talk, and her mother would say things like, "Dear, are you sure?" and "Do you really love him?" and "Does he make you happy?" and she would answer, "Yes, yes, oh yes." She pursued the scene to this most unlikely ending as if her life and sanity depended on it; as if to imagine it long and hard enough would bring some semblance of reality to the situation in which she found herself, alone with this man who insisted on being tender, and all the while, underneath, she heard the ugly and uncompromising beat of a distant war drum, warning her of some chaos or terror to come.

She dragged his suitcase to her side of the bed and unzipped it. Two shirts, two pairs of slacks, two pairs of boxer shorts. The shirts were starched and folded neatly, fresh from the laundry. She took out one of his shirts and smelled it, then unbuttoned it and eased it over her shoulders. It felt good. The trousers would be too wide and too short, certainly. Never mind. She could tie them up with her red scarf. She did so, and looked at herself in the mirror. She touched her lips, which were rouged from abrasion. I look exactly like a woman who has spent the day in bed with a strange man, and then borrowed his clothes, she thought. Except for the scarf, clearly a female thing, tied like a brazen scarlet sash around her waist. She was too old to be running about without a bra. But she liked the way her nipples bled through the surface of the cotton when she moved a certain way. She liked it very much. He had called her a beautiful woman. A man might say that to his whore. It had nonetheless moved her.

"I'm a beautiful woman," she said aloud, but softly, so he couldn't hear. She turned to the left side to gaze at herself in the mirror, and then to the right. "Oh, don't you see how beautiful I am?"

"I see it," he said.

She folded her arms across her breasts as if she were naked instead of fully clothed.

"The clothes," he said. "They suit you."

She neither explained nor apologized, but instead found her shoes under the bed and put them on, not looking at him.

"I suppose you do this sort of thing all the time," she said.

"Not all the time. And anyway you know it's not the same."

"That's what people like to tell themselves. That it's not the same. That somehow what they are doing isn't sordid, and exploitative, and meaningless."

She laughed.

He stood apart from her, leaning to one side perhaps, or at any rate he seemed to her to be slightly off-balance.

"Don't do that," he said.

She looked at him.

"Don't act as if nothing meaningful has happened here," he said. "Even if you believe that to be the case, please allow us to pretend otherwise."

She found her wallet in her purse and transferred it to her trousers pocket. "We can kill the time all right," she said. "Sixteen hours or so until checkout time. It's not so long. It's a lifetime, really. You're right. A lot can happen in sixteen hours. Even something meaningful."

He drew her up and tried to kiss her, gently, on the forehead. Momentarily confused by his tenderness, she turned her head away.

He let go of her again.

15

When he came into the room he found her staring at herself in the mirror. It was rare that his wife would be so accepting of herself, so able to overlook her physical flaws and delight in her body. "I'm a very beautiful woman," he heard the widow say, and felt in some small way that he had helped her to realize that truth. When she saw him standing there she grew fussy and embarrassed, making him want to hold her and soothe her again. He felt her body stiffen in response to his kiss. It provoked him. He had not expected her to reject him on any level, now that they were lovers, now that she had given up her last defense

to him. They were lovers! Did that not change everything? Did they not have some level of deeper understanding that transcended the particulars? Now that
they were fully clothed again she acted as if they had no
more intimacy between them than two people passing
on the street. It was his own fault. He had suggested
they go out for a while. If he had been ten years
younger he could have rutted her over and over again
without regard for his poor cock, which as it happened
now needed rest, and that's all he was worried about,
really, damn the thing, he needed some excuse. He
wasn't about to face that embarrassment. His cell
phone was ringing. How could that be? There was his
phone, by the side of the bed, ringing. He was certain
he had turned it off. She looked at him as if to say, See?
I know you. He felt himself dissembled into some
other thing, no longer lover, but husband, adulterer.
For of course it would be his wife. Four, five, six rings
now. The widow stared at him.

"Aren't you going to answer it?" she said.

He was dumbstruck. He did not want to answer the
telephone. He did not want to have his incidental life
encroach on the present, on his time with her. He held
her tightly, by the elbows, momentarily overcome by
the notion that she might try to answer it herself.

The phone stopped ringing.

"Shall we go, then?" he said.

"Why didn't you answer it?" she asked.

"You know why," he said.

He sank onto the bed again. She stood above him,
looking down, astonishingly serene. The room felt

stuffy and disheveled, as if he had stumbled into some other person's room, someone who didn't yet know how to take care of himself. Her face, looking down at him, was so open, so disarmingly open, that he could feel her eyes peering through him as if through an open window, to the depth of his shame. Her stillness was a kind of winter to him, not unkind, but unfeeling nonetheless.

"Shall we go, then?" he said again.

16

She allowed the Muslim to lead her down the hallway, absorbed by the pendulum-like weight of his hand in hers. He was the only man of his kind who had ever touched her. At times she imagined that she could glimpse a kind of primitive and barbaric beauty in his features, a fierceness, and it exhilarated her to be so close to its source. It helped not to look at him too closely, or to think about her motives too directly. As they walked she could feel herself falling into the role of joyful lover after first sex, enjoying the flush of her cheeks, the sway in her hips, the fullness in her center, still engorged and abraded from their lovemaking. Another self, equally vital, found that the touch of his fingers in her hand was unfamiliar and frighteningly potent, almost unpleasant in its intensity. Still a third self watched from some safe distance, entirely disassociated from the body and its choices. Where did her true self reside, then? She couldn't say. She felt as if, were they only to choose one hallway over another in their journey, she would be a different person at the end of it. She held his hand casually and gave no sign of her inner turmoil. What her friends would say! She would tell none of them, of course, except perhaps the one who had made a sexual career out of sleeping with foreign students, who had slept her way through the entire African continent and was now halfway through Europe; although even with this most adventuresome of her friends, the details would need to be altered. She would need to say the Muslim was a German or a Brazilian, to avoid the shock of it, the perversity of it, in which case it hardly mattered whether she said anything at all. A wave of shame overtook her, to touch that bright truth, that she was doing something so dishonest, so questionable, that she couldn't speak of it with even the least morally demanding of her friends. What was the good of it all, if it could never be mentioned again? In the morning she would be as alone and confused as ever. This observation left her feeling transparent and cheap, and she pulled her hand away from his and followed behind, not touching him. The hallway narrowed, then opened into the lobby, which looked somewhat less shabby and neglected at night, although empty, except for the thick-fingered man she

had seen at dinner the night before, who stood in front
of the dining room next to his girlfriend, peering into
its black interior. She followed the Muslim as he
walked near to where the man and his girlfriend stood,
and, just like the three of them, peered through the
closed glass doors.

"'Snot open," the man said.

She could see now that the woman with him was
much younger than he, even more so than she had
thought in the dim light of the dining room the night
before. Tonight instead of a business suit the thick-
fingered man wore a crimson-colored polo shirt. He
had thinning hair that fell across his forehead and a
pale, simple-looking face, and was drunk in that nearly
functional way of habitual drunks. The girl had a no-
nonsense, clinical air about her, like a physical educa-
tion instructor or nurse.

She stared into the dining room, perplexed to find
herself in such company.

"I wonder if they remembered to feed the fish," she
said.

The Muslim walked away and she found herself
alone with these other two, these strangers, these
countrymen. She didn't know whether to follow him
or to hang back. She watched as he traveled across the
lobby to the front desk, where a hotel employee sat behind the counter, spinning himself back and forth on a
high stool while staring at the opposite wall and breathing through his mouth. She decided to follow him.

"Will the dining room be opening tonight?" she
heard him say.

"Cook got sick."

"Then can you recommend a restaurant? Perhaps in town?"

The man opened a drawer and got out a pad of paper and a pencil. He stared at them both, holding his pencil to his lips, as if trying to decide what sort of food would suit them. Then he wrote down an address, ripped off the sheet of paper, and slapped the paper on the counter.

"Good place," he said. "Local specialties. Crab. Chowder."

"Good place?" The Muslim picked up the paper and studied it. "We want it to be good," he said.

"Very good," the man said. "Local specialties. People like you, you'll love it."

The man on the stool looked in her direction, then returned to spinning himself back and forth on his stool. His look reminded her of something unpleasant that had happened recently, although exactly what she could not say. The image of a neighbor came to her, the neighbor two doors down who was always accusing her and her husband of leading their dog to shit and piss on his lawn. He would apparently wait by the window until they came along, at least it seemed that every time they passed he would throw open his door and come flying down his front walk, insisting on showing them the little piles on the lawn, after which he would point out the circles of dead grass, at which point they would agree that someone's dog had, indeed, been at it again. Of course it was not their dog. Their dog did no such thing. Her husband explained it all to the man many times. He took care to never let the dog place one paw on the man's wretched patch of lawn. When she was alone she took to walking on the other side of the street whenever possible, until her husband said, Ridiculous, this is your street as much as his. Even after the dog died the hostility lingered. And then her husband died, too, and sometime after that she had walked by this man's house and had seen him at the window, and quite without expecting it from herself had walked up to his door and rung the bell, and when he answered she told him, You were always very mean to us for no reason, and now my dog is dead, and my husband is dead. The neighbor's face had become transparent with grief and sincere regret. For one brief and shining moment she stood there and savored her power over him. She could have smiled. She could have absolved him. Instead she turned and walked away, leaving him there to consider his sins. Now this man, spinning on his stool, seemed gratuitously hostile, in the manner of that neighbor and his piles of shit. Why was he singling her out, staring at her, as if judging her? She hadn't even been part of the conversation. She hadn't asked him for help. Perhaps she had imagined it.

"We could go into the town," the Muslim said. "This fellow has recommended a place in town where we can get dinner."

The thick-fingered man edged closer, pulling his girlfriend with him by the hand.

"Could you give us a lift?" the man said. "We've been having some trouble with the car. We can walk back along the beach. No trouble to you."

She knew he would say yes. He was that kind of man.

"All right," he said.

"Much appreciate it," the man said.

As the four of them walked two by two she saw her own car in the lot, a little farther off, parked where she had left it, and marveled at how familiar it looked. The man walking along with her looked familiar, too, in a way that she had not yet defined. The simple act of walking with a man, any man, was familiar. They made their way across a nearly vacant lot to his car, a slate-colored two-door sedan. He unlocked the doors. The other two climbed into the back seat. She sat down in front, next to him. He backed out and began his way down the hill, toward the main road. A cat or some other small animal ran along the top of a Dumpster at the edge of the lot, its eyes glowing back like head-lamps.

"Tight fit back here," said the man in back, and laughed, and belched. "Don't worry about moving your seat up, though. We'll adjust."

"I'm sorry."

"It's all right, really," said the man. "Beggars can't be choosers. That's what I always say."

The road dipped steeply and the light from the hotel behind them winked out, leaving only the illumination of his headlights on the trees to shield her from the utter dark, which seemed to close tightly around the car. Somewhere below them through these dense trees was a town, and she presumed more light. She remembered the eyes of the animal on the Dumpster, until all she could think about were all the other animals staring at them from the dark. It was the year for rabid squirrels. For frogs born with too many legs. A cougar that summer had attacked a toddler who was playing in his own backyard; the child was saved only when his mother beat at the animal's jaws with the bedsheets she had been hanging on the line, the only thing she could think to grab up in her frenzy to defend her child, and, miraculously, the beast gave up and ran away. She imagined the terror of the mother wielding her sheets and felt her own arms grow weary with the effort. She thought she could see the eyes of wild animals skittering past, just beyond the headlights. She looked at the man next to her and saw that he was smiling tightly, concentrating on the road ahead.

"Oh no, no, no," said the girl in the back seat.

"She's getting shy on me," the man announced. "Acting coy. She's thinking about leaving me."

"I'm not," the girl said. "You make up stories just to amuse yourself."

She felt the man paw her shoulder from the back seat.

"I'm putting her through college," he said.

"That explains it," the Muslim said.

"We aren't really fighting," said the thick-fingered man. "Anyway, I think it's good to fight. Me and my wife, we never used to. Eleven years and not a single harsh word between us. One day I come home and find her screwing a Mexican. His name was Cesar. Fuck that Cesar. Fuck him."

"It must have been very terrible for you."

"It's okay. Thank you. At first every day was shit. After that I sort of turned my life around, you know. I got into animal health care products. You wouldn't believe how much money there is in animal health care products. All through the divorce it was Cesar this, Cesar that. Cesar bought your daughter a bicycle. Cesar bought an eighty-dollar bottle of champagne for my birthday. Fuck him. I don't hold a grudge."

"Sure, baby," the girl said.

"No. Really. Because now I have it all. Money. Sex. True love. God, yes."

He let out a sound that may have been a snort, or a sob. She felt his paw on her shoulder again and coiled away.

"That's what you two lovebirds have, I guess," he said. "How about it, you two? Is it true love?"

"True love," said the Muslim.

He had only parroted the words of the thick-fingered man back to him. And yet when she looked at him again he seemed momentarily transformed, heroic. He did not look at her. She would not ask him later what he had meant. It was the kind of statement that would only be ruined by close examination.

"You're lucky," the man said. "I saw it in your eyes. Isn't that right, little poontang? Didn't I say the moment these two showed up, 'Baby, those two have the light of true love in their eyes'? Hang on to that feeling. Cherish it. Never will you find such a blessed thing in your life as true love. Say, what are you, a Mexican?"

He pulled at the Muslim's sleeve, then snorted again, or laughed. The Muslim drove with his head lowered, his hands gripping the wheel tightly, as if bracing for some looming hazard in the road. She hesitated, then touched his knee.

17

The road was dark, almost as if the air itself were opaque. He drove slowly and said little. The man in back droned on. It helped to think of the words as random noise, a white hum. He answered periodically, hardly aware of the murmurings coming from his lips. Even after decades of living in an English-speaking country he found there were times when he could will himself to hear the language as sounds only, empty of meaning, and thus protect himself from any meanings he preferred not to have leach into his mind. It helped to have the widow sitting next to him. He looked at her periodically as they drove. She looked as if she were waiting for her moment to open the car door and flee into the night.

"What are you, a Mexican?" the man in back said.

A finger poked him in the shoulder. He felt a spike of something like fear, to hear how the man's voice had eroded so quickly into something flat and sinister, where a simple question sounded like a threat. What a joke! To be mistaken for a Mexican by a man who hated Mexicans, and to be afraid to tell him the truth lest he incite some other unpleasant reaction! What a joke! He felt a sudden sweat and helplessness, all mixed up in a desire to accommodate, to be friends with this man, with the American man, and he hated himself for it.

"Not that I have anything against Mexicans," the man went on. "Except the one that was screwing my wife. All through the divorce it was Cesar this, Cesar that. Fuck that Cesar. Fuck him."

The threat passed. The man droned on. No reply would be required, no need to announce himself as any particular sort of person, from any particular place. He felt the widow's hand on his knee, her attempt at a consoling gesture. She, too, had asked him about his origins, of course, just that evening, and also when they had met. Many years earlier he had grown weary of this peculiarly American question, the way it encompassed not only the person's desire to know an address, the name of a town, and by that information to begin forming a wordless idea of someone, but also a yearning toward the other place, the mystical, longed-for homeland, the true home, the anchor from which one could never drift, even after living for years in a country where identity shifted as often as the tides, where an actor could become president, a window washer a hero. How these Americans longed for an ancestral home where nothing ever drifted! What they couldn't understand was that home was lost. It didn't exist any longer. Even the idea of home was tired and sad these days, and unnecessarily sentimental. And lately there was a new edge to the question, the curiosity now mixed with fear. How natural it had become to be hated! He had ignored that truth, bowing to the wishes of those around him, trying to become invisible, not the sort of person that would attract attention or remark. In stores the young, pimpled clerks dropped his change onto the counter to see his hands scrabbling after the nickels and quarters, to hear his own voice apologizing for it. The smirks, the unfinished sentences. Even worse than the snubs and aggressive acts from these strangers was the way his friends treated him, his friends, with their stupid politics that they always wanted to discuss with him, to show him that they understood, including him in their conversations as they would invite a person with some horrible, terminal disease, so they could feel good about themselves, so they could feel Christian! And even this widow, this strange, extreme woman next to him, had chosen him only for this reason, to hate him even as they loved one another, to experience his body as forbidden fruit, something to be eaten and thrown away, not human at all. Or perhaps to forgive. He couldn't say.

Now she sat apart again, not touching him, the gearshift separating them, both hands resting in her lap. The two in back had also fallen silent. They reached the town, and the main road now stretched before him like a procession of streetlights in the dark. He drove on. A crowd of men fanned out from a corner bar and onto the sidewalk, beer bottles in hand, music thumping. He stopped for a red light at the next intersection, where four men ran in front of the car. The last one slapped the hood as he passed, his face frozen momentarily in demonic relief by the headlights. Then they disappeared into the night. The light turned green and the car moved forward. The air in the car seemed too close to him. He opened his window and was relieved to smell the sea. A few blocks later he recognized a street name from the address the man at the hotel had given him, and turned into it gratefully. He drove over potholes, past mobile homes surrounded by chain-link fences hung with dead roses that were lit up by his headlights, and then fell into dark once more. A dog ran along a fence and barked at the car, incessant hacks. He drove slowly, inching ahead, diligently searching the porches and curbs for street numbers and finding none. He looked up and saw what could only have been his destination, several blocks ahead. A neon light in the shape of a crab, massive and vulgar, thrust itself above the surrounding roofs, flashing as it opened and closed its pincers. When he drove closer the light from the sign seeped into the car until it made her flash red with an artificial warmth. She looked up at the sign and said nothing. He turned into a dirt lot full of cars, found a place near the back of the lot, and shut off the engine.

"This is it," he said.

"So. This is it," said the man in back.

"Wait a moment," he said.

He opened his door and got out and walked around to the other side of the car, to open her door for her. He took her hand.

"Oh, that's very kind," she said.

Her mouth stretched into a vague smile as she unfolded herself and stood up. The man and his girlfriend followed, climbing over themselves and the seats and laughing at how stiff they were. The two of them lingered, standing next to the car, as if waiting for him to begin walking so they could follow. Why would they not be on their way? He resolved to ignore them. He put his arm over her shoulders, firmly, but awkwardly, as she was perhaps as much as an inch taller than he, and began to lead her toward the entrance. Holding her this way gave him a reassuring sense that he was in control of their progress. By increasing his pace he managed to create a distance of some yards between them and the other couple.

"Oh, stop," he heard the other girl say. "Stop, stop! Why do you have to behave like this? In a parking lot, for goodness' sake. What am I supposed to do with you?"

A squeal of a laugh followed. The door of the restaurant opened and an elderly couple came out, followed by a woman pushing a stroller through the door while her husband held it open. The baby in the stroller gazed up at him with solemn eyes. It startled him to see a child in the context of his adulterous event.

"I have heard of this place, you know," he heard the man who hated Cesar say. "Good place. Crab and chowder. All you can eat. It's in the guidebook. You pay first, then eat all you want. Extra for drinks. I read about it."

They joined a line to a cash register.

"I hate these kinds of places," the man's girlfriend said, and stroked at her hair, and touched her flat stomach with the palm of her hand, throwing her shoulders back and lifting her chin. She looked about as if searching for a party of friends she had expected to meet her there. He felt momentarily sorry for her. Then he noticed that her breasts were abnormally large for her frame, and was ashamed of himself for noticing.

"I hate these kinds of places because I always feel I have to stuff myself to get my money's worth," the girl said. "It's disgusting."

"Go ahead, it's my money," said the man. "You eat like a bird. You always do. She always does."

The man spoke these last words as if standing on a stage. Exactly as if he had stepped out of character for a moment to address the audience directly. Could he not see that no one was interested in his petty problems and triumphs? Fortunately they had reached the head of the line. He paid for two, then took the widow by the elbow, leading her into a low-ceilinged room of cramped tables filled with people wearing bibs with large red crabs printed on them, eating crab legs from huge stainless steel bowls. He led the widow through the crowd, to what seemed to be the only empty table. This was not what he had intended. The size and random anonymity of the crowd distressed him. He had imagined the two of them somewhere small, intimate, and dark. Here, in this cavern of a dining room filled with people, he could not help thinking that they would run into someone they knew. Someone would recognize them. He should have stayed with her in the hotel, not come out here for everyone to see them. The sound of voices and clattering utensils echoed from the walls, until he could hear nothing more than a loud and restless hum, a hive. He pulled out a chair for her, bumping the chair legs of a man sitting immediately behind, who shifted and twisted in his seat in an exaggerated way before looking up, his mouth open in silent protest. He apologized to the man. Then he also sat, feeling cowardly, afraid to break their personal silence amid the noise. He realized he still held his billfold in his hand. His pants had recently grown too snug to put his billfold away comfortably if he wasn't standing up. He was reluctant to stand up again, to make that fact known to her. Instead he placed the billfold deliberately on the table next to his napkin, then gave it a pat, as if to reassure himself. He unfolded his napkin and put it in his lap and smiled at her. She smiled back. They might have never been lovers. She was a peculiar woman. He covered her hand with his. After a long look that made him feel his discomfort she spoke to him.

"Here I am, wondering what to say to you," she said. "That's very strange how shy I feel. Considering."

She almost had to yell to be heard. Her admission touched him. He wanted to compliment her in some way, to say something that would make her feel at home with him.

"I should say you know me very well now," he said. "Better than anyone here. You needn't worry about saying anything in particular."

She looked relieved. He was also relieved. It gave them little need to speak further. They could just sit and hold hands, and eat, and leave.

He willed himself to relax. He could discern no single word in the babble, no train of a sentence, only an oppressive, ceaseless hum. He tried to find sense in the noise. "What, you dye your hair?" he heard, before the hum came back and covered over any other sound that he could recognize as speech. The widow was now rubbing her thumb in concentric circles on the palm of his hand.

"Are you happy?" he said.

"I'm very happy," she said. "I'm not going to think about it any more deeply. It gets in the way."

She gave his hand a squeeze and looked away, as if he had intruded and she was embarrassed to have been found out. His eyes were captured by the motion of an old man's face at another table. The man's jaw moved up and down, up and down, like a piston. A bowl of crab pieces appeared on their table followed by two bowls of white chowder. He tasted sand and said nothing.

"It's not like I've ever done this before," she said.

"Well, you shouldn't worry," he said. "Everything is fine."

Impulsively he leaned over and kissed her on the mouth. She smiled, then looked all around at who might have seen the kiss. He himself was shocked that he had done such a thing. He was not one to make such gestures in public. He willed himself to look like someone who would kiss a woman whenever he felt the urge. He could feel a thin film of sweat forming on his face. He closed his eyes and tried to concentrate. They would eat, and they would go back to the hotel. They would finish what they had come for. He opened his eyes again and found himself watching the movement of a crimson-colored shirt making its way through the crowd to this very table, yes, to this very table, his girlfriend trailing behind.

"I know you lovebirds would rather be alone," the man said. He sat, leaving his girlfriend to struggle alone with her own chair. "But see, here's the only empty two chairs in the place," he said. "People park themselves and eat until they're sick. It's the American way. Let's dig in."

The widow's hand receded from his. He felt a tension in his ribs that grew stronger as the other man grabbed a claw and began to work on it. The widow also began to eat, but delicately, after picking up a pair of tongs and searching out the smallest and most discrete bits of crab from the bowl to transfer to her plate. She cracked a leg and put the meat into her mouth.

"So, how did you lovebirds meet?" the man said.

"We've known one another forever," he said gruffly, to spare her any need to explain.

"That's the way true love is," said the man. "It lasts forever. If it doesn't last it wasn't love to begin with."

"That's beautiful," said the girl.

"I thought my wife loved me," said the man. "That's why I didn't get angry with her. I just dealt with the Mexican, *mano a mano*. I said look. This is America. We got laws. My wife is like my property. Touch her and I can legally kill you. So stay away. She loves me, you fuck. Not you. I took a swing at him and he went down. My wife took his side. That's when I knew. Not true love. Seven years ago now. Seven fucking years. Fuck that Cesar. Where's my chowder?"

He stood up, and threw his napkin on the table and walked away, as if momentarily stepping out of his re-curring role as cuckold. It was evidently a performance he could now do by rote and therefore avoid the te-dium of thinking new thoughts. The girl waved a fly from their table. Her eyes were cool, steady. She rested her elbows on the table and shrugged.

"He really is putting me through college," she said. "Last year he took me to Mazatlán. I want to assure you that generally speaking he really has nothing against Mexicans, señor."

The three of them sat in silence for what might have been several minutes, until the man appeared again, an apparition, his protruding stomach now covered over with a paper bib. He carried a pitcher of beer in one hand. In the other he carried four mugs. He plopped the beer and mugs down on the table and fished three more paper bibs out of his pocket, which he passed around.

"Fuckheads ran out of chowder," he said.

He poured himself a beer from the pitcher, too fast, mostly foam.

"Here's to you two lovebirds," he said, raising the mug and smiling broadly. "Help yourself."

"I don't drink."

"You don't drink? He doesn't drink?"

The man stuck his lip out, and nodded, slowly, as if forming an opinion, then leaned over until his face was very near to the table and stared at his plate.

"Twelve-step program?" he muttered.

"Of course not."

"Of course not. Of course not. No need to get hot under the collar, bud." the man said. Then he straightened up, and smiled again, and took a drink.

"Don't be a pig," said the girl. "Pour us some."

"Right, ladies."

The man filled two of the mugs and handed them over. To his dismay the widow accepted this man's largesse, draining it quickly and holding it out for more.

"I want to tell you something," the man said. He cocked his head in the direction of the girl, then nodded his head meaningfully. "Her parents threw her out. Yes. On the street. Oh, the humanity!"

"I don't think these people want to be bothered with my little story," the girl said. "You shouldn't impose. It isn't right."

"Oh yes," the man said.

"That must have been very difficult for you," the widow said.

"Oh," the girl said. "It wasn't much. I slept in a car

for a while. I never got sick. I never did drugs. Other people, they couldn't believe it. Here's a survivor, is what they said. They called me a survivor. I never did drugs. That's what kills you."

"You're very brave," the widow said.

The thick-fingered man looked across the table at the widow, his eyes narrowed, his mouth drawn in a thin, long line.

"You, madam, are a philosopher," the man said.

"What an idea."

"No, no," said the man. "You are very deep. You think about things deeply. There is wisdom in you. You're an old soul. A survivor. I feel as if I know you. Yes. Exactly as if I know you."

A smile broke across his sharp features. "I do know you, I do." he said. "Say, it's the widow on TV, baby. Look at her. I can't believe it. It's the widow on TV."

"Oh God," the girlfriend said. "Oh my God." She shook her head. Her mouth hung open in an expression of exaggerated shock. "People like you. I don't understand how you do it. You're a pillar. An absolute pillar. We all lean on you."

"We're having dinner with a pillar," the man said. "The towel heads won't get away with it. I want your autograph. Yes. Oh yes. Don't argue with me."

The man ripped at the paper that covered their table and then searched his pockets for a pen, laughing at his good fortune. He gave up on finding a pen and went to the next table to ask for one. "The fucking widow on TV," he heard the man say to the people sitting there, before coming back with a pen and urging the widow to sign his scrap of paper, which she did. He stuffed it into his pocket.

"I'm drunk," the girl said. "You've done it to me again."

The man's arm reached out and pinched the girl's cheek. "You love it," he said.

He noticed then that the man's hands and fingers were shockingly swollen, that they bulged like sausages, and thought, Yes, that explains it, the man is fatally self-indulgent, a disease of the spirit, of the circulation.

"Your husband was a hero," the girl said, leaning toward the widow. "A genuine hero. A genuine, Jewish hero. Every time I think about it, I cry."

"Oh no," said the widow. "He wasn't like that. He wouldn't want you to think that way about him."

"Tell me about him," the girl said. "I want to know. I want to be able to tell my children."

"That's none of your business," he blurted out, and stopped, abruptly, wondering what it was he meant to say. His own voice sounded alien to him. He wasn't sure of anything at all. He could not be sure whether the widow actually felt how he assumed her to feel. She had given this man her autograph, after all. For all he knew she enjoyed being recognized, and would share her sufferings indiscriminately, with anyone who asked. He couldn't be sure. She hadn't told him. He only knew that he felt personally wronged by their intrusion, as if these two had been attacking a member of his own family. The widow sat there next to him. He could not read her expression. Was she embarrassed?

Had he embarrassed her? Why wouldn't she look at him?

"What are you, her friend?" the man said, and looked at him sharply, as if trying to place him.

"A friend," the widow said.

"Now wait a minute," the man said. "Now wait just a minute. A man friend. In a hotel."

"He's a friend," the widow said. "He's just a friend."

"A Mexican friend?"

"Now look, don't get excited," said the girl. "We're drunk. Don't get excited."

The two of them looked at him. He felt a thick inevitability cloud his mind.

"Not Mexican," he answered. "Persian."

"Persian," the man said. "Does that mean, like, from Persia? Part of Thailand?"

"He means Arab," said the girl. "Arab, from the Middle East."

"Arab," the man said. "My nephew died in the Gulf War."

"Not Arab," he said. "Persian."

But the man was no longer listening. No. Instead he was imagining a better, more heroic role for himself. Soon he would be able to stop talking about Cesar and tell everyone instead about the day he beat up a towel head. After all, he had expected something like this to happen sooner or later to him. He had been expecting it for months, for years. The way these people could collapse all differences and hurts into a single feeling, which could flare up and consume any innocent in its path.

"Come on," he said to the widow, trying to sound commanding, or at least sure of himself, but hearing instead that he was pleading and plaintive. "Let's go."

She looked at him at last. He was stunned to realize, in that moment that she looked at him, that he was no longer thinking of her as widow, or victim, or failed actress, or partner in an illicit tryst, but as someone very much like himself. A victim of random violence. The shock of it frightened and exalted him. She was herself, and he loved her. He felt his love for her hover about them for a moment, fortifying them both, protecting them from the harsh and ugly light in which they found themselves. Then he felt his love expand until it filled up the space inside the room, and from there it radiated outward, to the people of this town, to the very ends of the earth and all its sufferings, all of which seemed to be represented by this grieving woman's eyes.

The man's fist now gripped the handle of his beer mug in a white-knuckled rage.

"To think I broke bread with you," the man said. "I feel like taking a fucking swing at you."

"Look, don't get upset," the girl said. She patted her man's arm, then turned to look at him across the table, frantic and conciliatory. "A boyfriend gave me a book of Rumi once," she said. "Let's all get along."

"Shut up," the fat-fingered man said to her. "Don't talk to him."

He stood up, but slowly, not wanting to precipitate the pending violence by any rash movement.

"Come on," he said to the widow again. "Let's go."

He felt a tightening in his chest that he would not call dread and he remembered why he hated crowds.

"That's right," said the fat-fingered man, rising partly out of his chair, his bib flapping under his chin. "Get out of here. You people are chickenshit cowards."

"Shut up yourself," said the widow. "He's a friend."

She rose at last and he grabbed her hand and led her away, toward the entrance. Not looking back. Not too fast. He could not help imagining that man rushing after them, knocking over chairs and pushing people out of his way in his zeal to take a swing at him. But he would not look back. He looked instead to the faces of the people they passed for any sign that they were being followed by a hostile force, and was thankful that the babble of the room continued on, and that the faces of those they passed stayed reassuringly slack.

18

They hurried through the parking lot to his car. The Muslim's hands were shaking as he unlocked it. The door of the restaurant opened and a band of light fell out across the parked cars and two women walked out. A high-pitched laugh, almost a cackle, carried across the parking lot to where they stood. He opened her door for her. Then he got in himself on the other side and locked the doors behind them. He spun out, drove a few blocks, and parked abruptly by the side of the road, where he began to beat on the steering wheel with his fists, over and over, until she was certain he would hurt himself, or her.

"Stop it," she said, at first softly, then louder, and louder again until she was yelling at him, frightening herself with the frenzy and terror she could hear in her own voice, and eventually he did stop. He leaned on the steering wheel with his face hidden in his hands. Then he straightened, with exaggerated dignity, and turned the engine off.

They were parked on some sort of side street. No one had turned on a porch light. No one had opened a door to investigate the sounds she was sure must have traveled out of their parked car before this. A streetlight down the road illuminated his hands on the wheel, but not his face. The hands in the light were miraculously unmarked. The dullness she had felt after her first beer had lifted, and all was clear and hard-edged again.

"I'm so very sorry," he said.

"It's all right. Nothing happened."

"You're right," he said. "Nothing happened."

The hands on the steering wheel moved to the face. He rubbed his temples and sighed.

"You need to forgive me," he said. "I don't feel quite up to driving for a moment."

"Of course."

Quite suddenly he began to beat on the steering wheel again and to say things incomprehensible to her, a guttural gibberish, and she was afraid. Reflexively, she began to console him or perhaps herself.

"There, there," she said. "It's going to be fine. Everything is going to be fine." "There, there." "You see? Everything is going to be fine."

He stopped, straightened again, his face receding into the shadows, and she heard him breathing in deep, measured breaths, to calm himself.

"I seem to have left my billfold on the table back there at the restaurant," he said at last.

"Your wallet?"

"Yes. My wallet."

"We'll go back."

"Oh yes. We'll go back and ask the gentleman with whom we were dining if he has seen it. No doubt he has already turned it into the front desk. With a love letter attached."

"We'll call the restaurant," she said. "They'll pick it up from the table for us. We'll go back in the morning. Perhaps they haven't noticed it yet."

"I suppose so."

They sat quietly now. She found herself experiencing a peacefulness, in that silence, that she recognized was quite out of place with the circumstances. Just now there was no shouting, no touching, no alarming events. Just now she could just sit and wonder. It could be that she was feeling superior to him. Her husband had never left his billfold on a table anywhere. He had never needed her help in any way. This man with her was now somewhat at the mercy of her beneficence. She found it a comforting and uplifting thought, to know that he would need her. It seemed that a long time passed in this restful manner.

"Whyever did those two need to follow us in there?" he said, more to himself than to her.

"I invited them," she said.

"You invited them?" His fingers in the light stretched out, then clenched.

"I'm sorry," she said. "It was when you got out of the car and came over to open my door for me. It seemed the right thing to do. I didn't know they would be like that. I was worried about what to say to you if we were alone."

"We were alone all afternoon."

"I was afraid of needing to speak with you in any detail," she said, and felt as if she had again said the wrong thing, that he would be offended. But he was reaching across to draw his hand along her forehead, in a way that she could only believe was gentle and loving.

"What the hell are you talking about?" he said, but softly, as if he were not angry; as if he really did want to understand her.

"I'm not a very good judge of character these days," she said. "I never know what people are thinking. I never know what they want from me. People do terrible things. Before that they live in neighborhoods. They make friends with neighbors like me. No one knows about them. I think about it too much. At times I begin to think everyone around me wants to hurt me. Then I realize how ridiculous that is, and I force myself to see the good in people. To think the best of them. Like the man we drove into town. Before he called you those names I thought, Poor thing. He has also lost someone he has loved. It can make you crazy."

"It has been very hard for you," he said.

"Oh, I don't know," she said. "I started taking Zoloft. I put on a lot of weight, it made me fat, but God, I survived."

"Don't do that," he said. "Don't treat me like I'm your audience."

"All right," she said.

"Tell me again why you invited me here," he said.

She felt dull, empty of any feeling.

"My husband used to tell me what to think about everything. I'm not complaining. I loved him. But without him I find I don't know what to think about things. You people all can't be bad. I know that. I wanted to prove it to myself. You must find me an ugly, bigoted woman."

"You're very good at that," he said. "At telling me exactly the truth, in a way that I will deny it."

"I don't know."

"No, I don't suppose you do."

He leaned toward her again, with his face in the light. Illuminated from above by the streetlight, his face looked like a mask. Then he grabbed both of her arms so tightly that it pained her, and he kissed her, deeply, in a way that seemed more primitive than revelatory. He let go of her just at the point when she was going to cry out that he was hurting her. He began to yank at her shirt with both hands until it was pulled out completely, then pushed up roughly at her bra until her breasts fell out below. He hunched over the gearshift and began to suck on her, and all the while great gasps came out of him. She marveled at her power. She felt as if she could hear the great heartbeat of the earth itself, pounding in her ears and rushing through the blood in her veins, as if she could feel the earth bucking and rolling through space. She was barely able to hold on. Look! She was alive after all! Not ash, but solid flesh! Here with this dark man crouched at her breast, she has found herself! She saw it all, and understood, with a piercing clarity that took her breath away before the fog came back and she was as confused as ever.

19

He watched her sitting there, alone, rubbing her lips with the back of her hand as if rubbing away a stain, and found himself empty of all judgment, of all will. He felt an overwhelming desire to comfort her, to shield her from life's disappointments, to make her happy, even; he felt as well the impossibility of it, the pretense of it, to think that he could ever offer anything real to her. His frustration rose until he found himself falling on her, pulling at her clothes until her breasts were exposed. He wanted desperately to touch her original self, before she had been so damaged by events. Her breasts tasted sweet. He felt the sweet shape of them in his mouth as sharply and vividly as he would something painful, and he grabbed at her with his mouth and sucked and tried to understand it until he needed to fall off of her as if coming up for air, and fell back into his seat, gasping and still not comprehending himself.

"Darling," he said.

She began immediately to tuck herself back together. She no longer looked exotic to him, but ordinary: beautifully, absolutely ordinary, as if she belonged there, sitting next to him, as if they had come to an understanding.

"My husband never grabbed me like that," she said.

He felt the rebuff in her words, and saw the husband as if standing in a fog, so thin that he seemed made of a dry, friable material, and so sad, and so absolutely perfect, so pure in death, with a hold on this woman that he could never influence in the slightest.

"I'm sorry," he said.

"Don't be stupid," she said. "I hadn't even meant to tell you about him. There are some conversations that don't belong when you're sleeping with someone you will never see again."

"I hate to think about that," he said. "I hate to think about not seeing you again after tomorrow morning."

He found it impossible, after that pronouncement, not to fall on her again, and when she blocked him from further access to her breasts he began to kiss her hair, over and over again, not hotly, like before, but with what he hoped would strike her as respect and tenderness, however awkward it was to caress her in his little car. He thought he felt her kiss him back. He felt her fingers grip at the back of his neck. When he stopped kissing her he looked into her face and saw that her eyes were closed. When she opened them again her expression was meek, a little embarrassed.

"I want to tell you about something," he said. "There was a moment there in the restaurant when I looked at you, and I felt that I could see you for who you really are. Not American. Not a widow. Not even female. But an individual, strong and lovely. My lover. I felt as if I understood you in all ways."

"But I am a widow," she said. "I am a woman. What can you be saying? What can you possibly be saying?"

"Just that we don't have to think of one another in such a limited way. We have this time together. No one knows us here. We can be anything to one another, if only for one night. Don't you think you can also imagine me in some other way?" he said. "As an individual? Not as a particular category? Even for a moment? For a night?"

She looked at him with what might have been disgust, as if what he had just said to her was so obscene that it had momentarily left her unable to speak. When she finally did speak it was in a hushed and reverential whisper.

"I want you to understand something here," she said. Her voice was low and gravelly. "When those men asked my husband if he was a Jew, he said, 'Yes, I am a Jew.' He didn't say, 'No, I'm an individual.' Do you understand what I am trying to say?" She lifted her head and smiled at him mirthlessly. "An individual.

What's that? Individuals are all the same, you know. Cut off from what they are. They are nothing at all. It's the context that matters. My husband was a Jew. Not a good Jew. But he gave up everything to acknowledge who he was. You are a Muslim. I am the widow of a Jew. That is who I am."

"No."

"Oh, you don't understand anything," she said. "I'm not complaining. It's who I am. It's what he was. I wonder, could you do that? Give up everything, your family, your life, just for once to be completely what you are? Could you do that?"

Her words had the wild, true clarity of a religious fanatic. The air rang as if from a tuning fork. He felt as if she was giving him a chance to redeem himself, as if she had asked him to make an irrevocable, right decision, a vow, that she was waiting there with wild eyes for his reply. He hesitated. He wondered briefly about her sanity. She said nothing more. And into the silence came a flooded awareness again of his surroundings. He heard some mundane argument going on in one of these houses. An engine started. The horrible sounds of incidental life descended on him. She shook her head and smiled.

"Never mind," she said. "It doesn't matter."

"So what am I to you?" he said. "Am I anything at all to you?"

She looked at him through the gloom. She nodded and touched his face.

"You're the first," she said.

"The first since your husband."

"Yes," she said. "I thought I knew what to expect with him. He was always the same. Every day with him. I was always the same. What did I know? What difference does it make? I'm so unhappy! I'm such an idiot!"

"No," he said. "No you're not."

"I am," she said. "I have terrible thoughts. For the longest time I've wanted to hurt a man of your sort."

The words came sighing out of her, an escaped gas, deflating her, leaving her face sagging and ghastly.

"What do you mean?"

"I don't know."

"Because of your husband."

"I think so. Because of the way we were. Because of what happened."

"And now?"

"I think so," she said. "To be in control. To see how it feels. I've never done anything like that before. It's what I wanted. Although I have never allowed myself to imagine it. All this time. Not until this very moment did I ever allow myself to imagine it."

Her face was now radiant and beautiful again, lit up in the glow from the streetlight outside the car. He was surprised to discover he was not disgusted by her admission. Not even unhappy. A tremor of joy and intense arousal rushed through him. To think that she had revealed herself to him at last, revealed herself in a far more intimate way than the mere act of taking clothes off, or making love together, or telling him in words the specifics of her loss! A chasm opened up before him, and instead of turning back he felt certain it was time to fly into it, to stop for once the burden of being a careful man. A voluntary helplessness animated his limbs and his mind. He wanted to touch her again, to show her by his touch that he understood. At the very least, he wanted to still the wringing hands, to smooth her turmoil with soft words and touches. But he did not reach out to her, after all. No. Better instead to give her time, to allow her to calm herself, without him imposing his will on her, without him deciding for her how she should feel. By restraining himself in this manner he felt superior to her husband, who had shown no such restraint, who had apparently told her over and over again how to behave and what to think. Better to allow her to find herself. The rightness of his actions filled him with contentment. He found his keys and put them into the ignition.

Before he could turn the engine there came the rise and fall of a siren, and an ambulance made its way past them, up the street and away. Immediately following the siren's decrescendo came the drone of low-flying planes overhead, close and low enough to set the car windows rattling.

"Something has happened," he said. "Some kind of emergency."

His hands rested lightly on the steering wheel.

"Yes," she said. "Something has happened."

They drove back to the hotel.

20

Since they had returned to their room a great shyness had come over them both, where every gesture was weighted with far more meaning than before. She had turned on a bedside lamp when they arrived, and closed the curtain, little housewifely acts accompanied by fussy gestures. He sat on the edge of the bed and called all the credit card companies that he could think of, canceling his accounts. He found himself enjoying the routine of dialing each number and speaking to these women with their emotionless, droning voices, who took care of him dispassionately, and who wanted nothing from him. The room looked like it was part of another man's life and age. And yet here it was, his own valise, right on the floor next to the bed where he had left it. After he was done with his telephone calls they took a shower together. She scrubbed him with the tiny bar of hotel soap, then positioned him under the spray to rinse him off. He felt the ages and the hours fall away until he was new again. She stooped and soaped him with the efficiency of a geriatric nurse. They didn't kiss. After she dried them both she found two hotel robes in the closet, vestiges of better times. She helped him into his robe. He watched her in the mirror as he sat on the bed. Her breasts were just the way he remembered them from that afternoon. Her skin and shape were familiar to him, but at the same time still alien territory, completely unfamiliar, as if she had made a brilliant duplication of herself sometime when he wasn't looking. A doppelgänger. A changeling. Except this woman here with him now, he thought, was the original; she had replaced the copy, not the other way around. She was a masterpiece of subtle shadings combined with violent and saturated splashes of color. No copy at all.

A buzz came through the walls, as from machinery, an elevator; otherwise the silence of an abandoned building. The lobby had been deserted. The stool behind the front desk sat empty of its former occupant. No sign of the old drunk and his girlfriend. The woman's eyes met his in the mirror before she bent her head and body shyly away from him and tied her robe shut.

"I feel like I've never been with you before," she said.

"We were different people then," he said, and believed it.

"Yes," she said. "Everyone changes."

She heated water in the little machine by the sink and made them both tea, flavoring it with artificial creamer. They sat on the edge of the bed, side by side, and drank out of paper cups. Their shoulders touched in the intimate way of new lovers.

"I'm afraid to begin again," she said.

She didn't look afraid. She looked poised and ready for all things.

"What are you afraid of?"

"I'm afraid that you will think I'm ridiculous," she said. "Or sick. I know you better now. You know me better now. It changes everything. It's frightening me how much your opinion matters to me."

"Yes."

Looking at her, he felt a dizzy vertigo and the room itself seemed to shake. I know you, he wanted to say. I know what you have suffered, because I have also suffered such a loss. If he had been less undone by the events of the evening he would have told her without hesitation, assuming that sharing his own loss would make her able to bear her own. But now, after losing so much of himself and his habits through his strange association with this woman, he understood that such shared intimacies are not really what she needed from him. She wanted to feel unique in her grief. She wanted

to feel called upon by the fates to bear a special burden.
So he said nothing. He bore his own memories silently
for once. A quiet emptiness opened up in his mind as
he sat there, into which, to his utter surprise, flowed the
image of his wife, proud, silent, immaculately dressed
and made up, mother to his children, loving spouse. It
occurred to him that his wife was neither shallow, nor
empty, but merely practicing forbearance, allowing
him to take up all the available space with his own sor-
rows and needs. How completely she capitulated to
him! Thinking about his wife in this way pleased him.
He was sorry for what he had done to her over the
years. He hoped to make it up to her. He wanted to
follow her example. He wanted to be of use. The
woman sitting next to him was in need of him now.
She seemed quite unable to gather herself together.
She was far away from him now, lost in her own
thoughts and terrors.

After a moment's stillness the shaking in the room
came once more, and he realized that the shaking was
real, a tremor in the ground, a tangible, real thing that
was happening to the two of them and the world at
large. Not enough to spill their tea, maybe. But enough
to move the liquid in his cup. The shaking stopped,
followed by a loud sound, a blast from some loud signal, perhaps from a firehouse, but somehow louder and
more diffuse.

"What can it be?"

"The end of civilization," he said.

"That happened already. Long ago."

"Well then, nothing to worry about."

"We could turn on the television."

"No."

"To find out, I mean."

"No doubt someone has flown a plane into a power plant around here."

"Nuclear?"

"Mm."

"You are terrible."

"Or anthrax," he said. "From the air. The planes we heard."

"Ricin," she said. "Smallpox."

"Killer bees."

"Men with knives."

"Not knives. Guns."

"Guns, yes," she said. "Shooting in the streets. I hear that's the way it begins. For the longest time after there is shooting in the streets the people just continue on like before, drinking tea and fucking."

The word she used startled him. It seemed crude and out of character for her.

"That's true," he said.

"You know it's true, I suppose," she said. "Because of what happened to you. Back home, I mean. It must have been something like that. To make you leave. To give you those bad memories you spoke of."

"But see, you're right, we're drinking tea, just as you say."

"Yes."

"So do you want me to fuck you now?"

The verb fell awkwardly from his lips. He felt fool-ish and unnecessarily melodramatic.

"No," she said. "I want you to close your eyes."

"Yes," he said, or tried to say, because his throat had closed.

So he nodded.

21

She watched him as he sat on the bed, his eyes closed, his breath coming in short bursts as if he were trying to control it, and failing. She began softly, by taking the robe from his shoulders. He kept his eyes closed. His obedience frightened her. To steady herself, she pretended that she was someone else, that she was watching herself from a distance. Now that his eyes were closed she had the opportunity to really look at him for the first time. He was always looking at her and making her look away. Now was her turn to be voyeur. His face was fleshy. It had a sheen of sweat over it, even now after they had just bathed. His nostrils flared as he breathed. Even now his face was like a mask to her. She had no imagination about what was behind the closed lids. A thickness about his neck and shoulders resolved itself into a broad chest covered with sparse, graying hair. He had placed one hand on each knee, as if wanting to stabilize himself and to calm his emotions, but his cock rose up between his legs as if to seek her out. His vulnerability moved her.

He opened his eyes.

"Don't do that," she said. "I told you to close them."

She slapped him on the chest and he closed his eyes again, but smiled, which enraged her; she flailed at him until he opened his eyes again and grabbed her wrists.

"Look, you need to be serious about it," he said.

"Close your fucking eyes," she said.

He closed his eyes. She sat on his lap. After a moment's deliberation she pushed her tongue into his mouth. She pulled back and looked at him. His eyes were still closed. His mouth was open, slack-jawed. He didn't move. She pinched both of his nipples, hard. The mouth closed, the jaw clenched, but he did not open his eyes or move away from her or make a sound.

She felt a sudden faintness, from which she recovered by chewing on her inner cheek.

She walked back into the bathroom and found the trousers she was wearing earlier, still on the floor where she stepped out of them before their shower, and picked them up. She untied her scarf from where she had knotted it around the trousers to use as a belt, long ago, earlier that evening, before they went out. She returned to the bedroom and was pleased to see that he had neither moved nor opened his eyes. She climbed around him on the bed and covered his eyes with the scarf, gently, first brushing it over his face so that he could breathe in her scent and be assured that she meant no harm.

"Is it all right?" she asked.

He nodded.

She knotted the scarf over his eyes.

"I love you," she said.

She found his belt and, after some deliberation, decided to cinch it about his ankles. That left only the hands. She looked around the room, in his bags and in hers, for some sort of binding device, before finally finding a cheap wire hanger in the closet, behind her navy suit that she had hung up so carefully that afternoon. She picked up the hanger and stared at it. Just a cheap wire hanger. Yet at that moment that ordinary household object made her hands shake. She stared at it, seeking answers. The inherent cruelty of ordinary things, she thought. A wire. A piece of string. A box cutter.

She turned her attention back to the closet and found two more hangers, far in the back, on the floor. Three hangers in the closet that weren't those silly, theftproof wooden ones without a hook. With difficulty she unwound each of them, one by one, slowly, and pulled them straight, while the shaking in her hands made its way up from her fingers to her arms and shoulders until her whole body shook. Her teeth rattled. The rest of her body had set to fluttering, yes, to fluttering, as if she were made of millions of tiny pieces each moving independently of the others. As if she were cilia. She walked back to the bed, carrying the long wires in her hands, watching them bounce and sway with each step, and sat down next to him on the bed. He looked wise to her, and unafraid. The blindfold over his eyes gave her the notion that he could see everything quite clearly, better than before.

"Have you done this sort of thing before?" she said.

"This? No. No."

"Neither have I."

She touched his knee, a question, and he nodded. She took his nod as permission to continue, which relieved her. She touched both of his hands with her fingertips, lovingly, and kissed their palms, before guiding them to the small of his back. For a few seconds the fingers behaved like creatures of their own will, flying away from the material that bound them. She patted at them as she would a cat, coaxing them to cooperate, to be at rest and at peace. She kissed his back. There, there. The fingers relaxed. She began to wind one of the wires about his wrist, terrified at the depth of her capacity to be cruel, now that she had been given permission. She had long suspected herself of being capable of such real cruelty. Here was a man she would never see again, never touch again, what difference did it make if she were to harm him? So it must be with suicides, she thought. The depth of their understanding is very great. To know they will never be held responsible for their final acts. To know they will be beyond the reach of any censure.

It was difficult to bend the wire to her wishes. It was not going to be pretty, when she was done. The man

breathed a ragged sigh. She began to twist a complicated pattern of figure eights about the wrists, working
diligently, grunting a little to pull the thick wires into
an acceptable arrangement, embellishing her work with
frequent, chaotic loops and twists. She took care to
complete her work with the ends of the wires out of the
reach of his opposable thumbs. She used two of the
hangers before she felt she was done. She sat back and
looked at her handiwork. Her own fingers felt exhausted from her labors. Although she had never had
an occasion to bind wrists before, it looked to her to be
a decent job.

"There," she said.

She said it close, breath-full, almost in his ear. He
inhaled sharply, a manifestation of his arousal. There
was no use deluding herself. She was excited, too. Although to call it arousal felt cheap. The colors of her
feelings ranged so far beyond the sexual.

"I love you," she said again.

She got up off the bed and stood several feet away,
near the bathroom door, watching him. At first he
made no move. After several minutes he began to lean
his head to one side, as if listening for her. Good, she
thought. Everything is good. She went into the bathroom and closed the door.

The air was still steamy from their shower. Their
clothes lay where they had dropped them. She picked a
used towel up from the floor and wiped the mirror
with it, looking at herself, deliberating the line of her
jaw. Her left eye had recently developed a small tic that
worried her. She watched the eye twitch in the mirror

as if it were some other eye, someone else who had the tic. Who was this woman? Sometimes she had caught a glimpse of herself in a shopwindow a few moments before she had known it was her own reflection. In these circumstances the woman who was her own image had invariably startled her, the intensity of her gestures and facial expressions making her seem utterly hideous and foreign. But now that she was looking at her face through the artifice of self-awareness, all was distorted and therefore bearable.

She let her robe drop to the floor and wondered if she had ever been so completely inhabiting her own body before this moment. Although the steam still warmed the room, she felt a chill. She slowly unzipped his shaving kit and took out his can of shaving cream. The razor was still perched on the edge of the sink where he had left it. Just as was her habit, she sat on the toilet seat and began with the left leg below the knee, shaving it smooth. Then the right. Then her upper thighs. She stopped. Had the terrorists shaved their genital area as well? She had heard no mention of it. Only the vague reference to the fact that they had shaved their entire bodies before their suicide acts, as part of their ritualistic cleansing. She watched as the razor made its way through foam she had smoothed across her inner thighs. Then, in an act that even in her agitated state she recognized as compulsive, she began to shave her crotch with slow and deliberate care, patch by patch, carefully, until it too was naked. She looked at the bareness between her legs and felt like she was looking at someone else's body. After she grew tired of gazing at herself in this manner, she reached inside and released her diaphragm, pulling it out. To her dull surprise a surge of menstrual blood followed. Time passed again. She had all the time, and time enough. After a while she turned her attention to her abdomen, covering her stomach with the shaving cream before swiping the blade across her middle from her crotch to her ribs in long, deliberate lines in the foam until she was clean of it. Then she covered her breasts and chest and neck with the stuff, and she gathered her strength, and finished the job, at last shaving the downy hairs from her neck and arms. Then she turned on the tap in the shower and stepped in, to wash away any stray hairs or shaving cream still clinging to her skin. The warm water flowed over her body, unimpeded by any covering whatsoever. She marveled at how different water felt than before, slippery and metallic, sliding across skin that had never before been so bare. The pain inside her intensified, then diffused throughout her body until every part of her felt the same drumming throb. Then she turned the water off, stepped out, and toweled herself dry.

22

When she first laid the blindfold across his eyes he felt a rough joy, strength, power even, to be acquiescing to her wishes so completely. Her requests still felt light and flirtatious, but he knew better. Even in these earliest of times he knew better. Some part of him was alarmed and startled and wholly unprepared for the passive way the rest of him accepted her desire to dominate him. He wondered if it was this fight between the will to resist and the will to acquiesce that drove all his decisions; a tendency that he was now experiencing in its most extreme expression. He inhabited a body that knew what it was giving up, to be bound in this way, by a woman who had never made her intentions fully clear. And yet. How enormous his erection grew, to be humiliated in this manner, to have her play out her grief on him! When she knelt and bound his feet together with what he knew to be his own belt he felt himself grow hard, who would have known? He couldn't see it with his eyes and he couldn't touch it, either, now that she had drawn his hands behind his back and continued her work of trussing him up, but he could feel his cock growing beyond all proportion to himself and his body until the rest of him was just some bit of cast-off skin because all the blood in his body had gone to his organ. He had heard of this sort of thing, of course. He had seen brazen, indelible images of women bound and gagged; seen the pornography his school friends had flashed at him; how they had smirked at his discomfiture! The erections then had embarrassed him. But now he found himself thrust into the scene with his entire body, no longer the voyeur, but the subject, how outrageous and wonderful it was! How exquisite! How perfectly intimate!

And then she left him.

In his state of intense agitation it wasn't clear to him whether he heard her leave altogether or if she merely opened the door to the bathroom and closed it behind her. In any case he had his erection to keep him company. He had the impression that he had never felt quite so happy with its company before, not even when he was young. His organ sang. All he need do, to maintain its steel-like hardness, was to think of her return-

ing, spreading herself as wide as possible to allow him
passage. At the slightest intimation of softening he
would think of her again, and all would be well. Time
passed. All he needed to do was think of her return. After a while it occurred to him that she had been gone
for some time, and when he tried this time to think of
her return, the thought instead crept into his mind before he could stop it that perhaps she would not be returning very soon. His erection collapsed. He passed
quickly through a stage of intense irritation with her
before he grew worried, then afraid. What if she wasn't
coming back? What if she had left him here, to be
found by some illiterate but hardworking and God-
fearing maid in the morning, him bound hand and
foot, and no billfold, no identification, an undesirable
alien of the sort that should be sent back where they
came from, yes, he was sure that had been her goal all
along, to humiliate him in this far less exotic way than
he had originally hoped. Perhaps she had planned it all
out. Perhaps she had a lover named Cesar. He had
fallen back onto the bed now, fallen back into his despair, and pushed himself along like a great worm until
he was lying across the length of it, on his side, since to
lie on his back meant to lie on top of his hands, which
were already numb and which chafed where the wire
had bound him too tightly. Was there no way to release
his hands? He tried and failed. Worse, an unpleasant
stickiness now covered the base of his palms. He found
himself preoccupied with an unrelenting desire to release his hands, so that he could feel his own body and
assure himself that it was his, still whole. Without the

ability to see himself or to run his hands along his skin, he grew obsessed with the notion that he was dissolving at the edges, no longer altogether there at all. Like other men, he had often played with the notion of surrendering so absolutely to another. He was finding the reality of it unbearable: first, to be sure, unbearably euphoric; but now unbearably desperate. At least she had neglected to gag him. He could call out if necessary. Then he remembered the long silent walk they had taken from the room to the lobby, hallways empty of all life, and despaired of ever being found again. He remembered his cell phone that lay on the table by the bed with some faint hope. Perhaps if he could just be sure it was still turned on. He had heard police could triangulate one's location just from a cell phone's activation. It seemed possible, if all else failed, that he could struggle his way over there and find a way to activate it, perhaps even to press a number at least on his speed-dialing menu, in case his triangulation theory was faulty, even with his hands bound. He thought of the numbers he had programmed into his cell phone and smiled at the thought of dialing any of them, trapped as he was in his current predicament. His wife. His boss. Oh, the explaining he would need to do! A laugh released him from his terror, leaving at last only an emptiness and fatigue, and a numbness in his hands. Then, boredom.

He fell asleep, where he floated on the edge of dreams so intense and erotic that they pushed him toward wakefulness, toward an awareness of his nipples rasping along starched sheets or of the nagging con-

stant pain circling his wrists, before dropping him back
into sleep once more. His dreams took on the vividness
of waking visions, taut and terrifying, more real than illusion, where he was not aware any longer of what was
truth, what a night terror. He dreamed of spying on his
mother through the gauzy plastic of a shower curtain
while she lathered herself, like any young boy might
spy on his mother, her turnings revealing a breast, a
bottom, before she was obscured by a wave of steam.
As he stared past the steam, trying to glimpse her
again, he became aware that she was not alone in that
shower; no, there was a bantam rooster in there with
her, its tiny organ erect and pointing at her like the
smallest finger while the bird crowed and sang and
flapped its strong wings, splashing water all about. The
oddity of that image of a bird in a shower stall pushed
him up closer to wakefulness. What did it mean? Had
he ever actually seen his mother bathe? He fell back
into a deeper slumber before he could answer himself,
into a dream in which he found himself in an airport,
watching as the widow carried a rooster under her arm
and walked away from him. He called to her. She didn't
turn, but the bird did, staring at him with its stupid
bird eyes, its neck elongating grotesquely before flattening again into its feathers, then elongating again; its
wattle hanging down and flapping uselessly. Still another dream flowed over this one and extinguished it,
and he found himself lying naked on a henhouse floor,
with thousands of birds pecking at him. I have heard of
this sort of thing, his dream-self thought. I have heard
of animals sometimes cannibalizing their own, when

they find themselves in desperate circumstances; even animals of an order far higher than these beasts. The pain increased until he was carried up once more to the edge of wakefulness, and then woke up entirely. After a moment's reeling disorientation he ordered his sensations into what they actually were: she was spanking him across the buttocks with something that gave him a small but undeniable bite at the end of each blow.

23

When she stepped out of the bathroom and into the bedroom she was momentarily afraid. It seemed as if the room were tilted more to one side than she remembered, that she might slide away entirely if she didn't step carefully. A single light shone from a lamp by the bed. The corners of the room were steeped in shadow. He slept, lying on the far side of the bed, facing away from her, his breathing soft and rasping. A strange affection welled up in her as she looked at him. He reminded her of herself, as she had been only that afternoon, when she had lain there naked and waited for him to come back into the room and violate her. His posture was so familiar to her that she could feel it as a memory in her own body, feel the press of the mattress against shoulder and hip as if she were lying there instead. It was not what she expected to feel, to feel as if it were she, there on the bed. Who was standing here, then? It seemed that for this anniversary she felt a need to inhabit every body, to understand every player. Herself. Her husband. Her husband's murderers. Who was this person on the bed? The instrument of her destruction, or her salvation. What division could be made between the two, after all? What difference between suffering and ecstasy, civilization and savagery, brutality and tenderness? He was everything to her now. How perfectly this man had attempted to please her! He could do more. She imagined him saying the last words to her that her husband had ever spoken. She felt a moment's weakness, remembering her husband's phone call. She had not known what to say to him, had not believed it, and none of it felt connected with her own life; she was only watching someone else's misfortune. Only later did her husband's words touch her. And then they never left her alone again.

She stood at the foot of the bed and memorized the curve of his buttocks. At this angle they looked womanly. Or perhaps it was the way he was tied, hand and foot, the way his hands behind his back made him raise his hips forward and up. He looked quite lovely to her. After gazing at him in this manner for some time she realized that he was dreaming: she heard him whimper. She would have him awake now. The desire to wake him seized her without warning. She found the third wire hanger at the foot of the bed where she had left it, stretched out into a long wand, and took it up in her hand, and began to tap him with it, lightly, across his buttocks. Then harder. The buttocks moved away and his breathing changed abruptly and she knew he was awake. She stopped and was still again, kneeling over him, kissing his temple and running her hand along his throat.

"You came back," he said.

"Of course I came back."

It occurred to her that she wanted him to feel her bareness. She straddled and crouched over him so that he could just touch her with the fingertips of his bound hands. She watched his fingers feel her. He breathed in sharply, exploring her new landscape in fitful grabs before she moved away and sat down on the bed next to him, cross-legged. She touched her bareness absently and considered what she might do next. His hips rose to find her again, alarming her. She moved farther away from him and arranged herself until she was once more sitting cross-legged on the bed, far out of his reach, and tried to decide. She was aware of time passing, of opportunities lost, moment following moment; nevertheless, she was unable to create any sort of forward momentum that would displace her inertia. She was defeated by a lack of will to continue what she had begun. She felt deeply her inexperience in such matters. The way she had trussed him, for instance, with his hands behind his back; it limited her options. She could not now turn him over and straddle him without forcing him to lie on his hands, which was too cruel for her even in her current mood; she felt faint at the thought of wires digging into his back, finding a kidney or other vital organ. Untying the hands felt all the more ridiculous, after all that work to wire them up to begin with. The great, meaty expanse of his rump still rose and fell, dark hairs covering it in a light moss.

"What are you going to do with me?" he said.

"Shut up," she said.

The voice startled her; her voice, but far deeper and more guttural than she remembered her own voice to be. She was annoyed with him, enraged; sure that he had interrupted her train of thought just when she had been on the verge of discovering some great truth. About him. About her. All irretrievably forgotten.

At a loss for what to do with herself next, she took up her wire and began to rap him across the flanks with it again, not hard, not too hard, but enough to draw a bead of blood with each downbeat. He moved fitfully back and forth across the bed, but didn't speak, didn't ask her to stop. She became aware that his movements produced an intimate, uncanny effect on her respiration; the simple act of watching him move back and forth in response to her taps had changed the cadence of her breathing. She could feel the blood pulsing through her veins, its pace accelerating with each touch of the wire, each bead of blood. And yet a certain formality had come over her senses. She felt as if she were performing a ritualistic duet with this man, that was, in its own way, as formal and as intricate as a court minuet. She watched the beads of blood appear across his buttocks, one by one. And still it did not seem to her that the man was particularly intent on avoiding the fall of the wire. If he had given any overt sign of protest she would have stopped, stricken and contrite. At the slightest protest from him, she would have been ashamed and disgusted with herself. She would have untied him immediately and begged his forgiveness. He was bent forward from the knees, his face on the bed and turned away from her, his hips high. Why did he not tell her to stop? She reached around to feel him and discovered his cock was engorged. Startled, she took her hand away. Her uncertainty increased, brought on by his unconcealed desire. She watched his hips rise and fall and wished fervently for some hard thing rising up out of her body so she could thrust it into him. She reached around and found his erection again and hated it. She squeezed him, hard enough to hurt him.

She put her wire down and kneeled behind him, straddling his shins, and put the palms of both hands on his buttocks. She thought of a woman's hips. She touched his asshole lightly with a fingertip, shocking herself with her boldness. As her finger touched him, he stopped breathing. She did it again, and noticed the same result. She couldn't understand it, either how it aroused her or how she could not have known before this time in her life that it would arouse her to touch a man in this way. Even the smell of him aroused her, as it seemed to her more intimate than anything she had known before, that he would be opening to her in this way. She reached around again to hold his cock, then pushed a finger into him; then two. His erection fell

and he cried out, cunt, piss, fuck, some throaty wan-
derings after that. Hurt, and yet even now he seemed
to open to her, as if she really did have a cock, as if she
really were fucking him with her own cock at that very
moment and as if he liked it.

"Do you still want to understand me?" she said.
"Yes."
"Tell me you like this," she said.
"Yes."
"Say, 'I like this.'"
"I like this."
"Tell me not to stop."
"Don't stop."
"What do you feel?"
A pause.
"Like a woman," he said.
"Cunt," she said. "Fucking cunt."

His ass was now slippery and open to her. This is
what men think when they make love to us, she
thought. What I feel now. Wanting to hurt her, invade
her, to rip her apart. And my lover's only purpose is to
allow it. This is what this man thought of me, at the
moment of his orgasm. This is what my husband
thought of me, at the moment of his orgasm. Wanting
to penetrate. And look how he asks for it! She was so
dumbfounded by it that she fucked him deeply, not
even aware that she was also clawing at herself until she
came.

24

He felt her fall off of him. His anus burned. His shoulders were wrenched out of their usual position; his wrists sang with a sharp pain all their own. He imagined his wrists must now be covered with raised welts from the wire and its chafings. He felt crude and animal. He was afraid to speak. His erection had returned, with greater force. How could it be aroused? His penis felt detached from the rest of the body and its intentions. For a moment all was quiet. Long enough for him to feel anxious, to feel a long flash of fear and lust and giddy passion course through his body, leaving him helpless and needing more.

"Who are you?" she said.

He did not recognize the voice. He tried to see through the gauze of her scarf; the light of the bedside lamp bled through like a red sun.

"Who are you?" she said again, and she slapped him across his face, and slapped him again when he didn't speak, and after the third slap he thought that he understood what she wanted of him, and that he also understood himself.

"I am a Muslim," he said.

He heard her sigh.

"Do you want to go on?" she said.

He was confused. Did he have a choice? He felt he had no choice. The illusion of choice had been stripped away, leaving him unable to pretend any longer that he could choose. He waited for her to take pity on his misery and helplessness. He waited for her to release him. He imagined her face, sorrowful, merciful, the memory of her morbid pallor somehow lovely to him even now, releasing him from his bonds and washing him with her tears. He may have nodded.

Nothing happened.

Suddenly she was on him again, breathing in his ear. Something cold and long and metallic found its way around his neck; the wire. He heard guttural, choking sounds, his own. Then the wire fell away and he could breathe again. She pulled his head back by the hair, exposing his neck once more. He felt a jab of something sharp at his throat near the left ear; she had broken skin. The dull knowledge finally fell on him, that he hadn't ever known her at all; he felt himself fly away until all that was left was a beast that was blessed with no imagination of the future.

"Tell them to fear us," she whispered.

The words rattled in his mind, familiar, the rhythm of them. Of a videotape of her husband's last moments. He had seen it, over and over again, on the evening news, on the morning news, on the Internet, inescapable for three weeks solid and even after all this time played now and then for various anniversaries and made-for-television documentaries. Without being able to help himself he had grown familiar with the voice of the blindfolded man, the husband, the man with his hands tied behind his back, saying his last words to his wife in that grainy loop of film. As familiar as he had become now with her own voice. He discovered that his teeth were chattering, a physical tremor of the lower jaw that he was helpless to stop. Did all frightened men feel as cold as this? He forgot to wonder because she was choking him again; then released the tension at his throat once more. His erection remained. His body trembled deeply. He had the shakes. Terror and lust, together. The same. We are poised on the edge, he thought. A moment like this comes just before taking vows. Just before dying. Committed, but not yet set in motion. He understood it now.

"You can't imagine what a release it is," she said. "To know yourself. That irrevocable moment when you lose everything else."

She grunted and leaned away from him, and then she was back, terrifying him now, pulling his head up by the hair. He felt her press his cell phone to his ear. "No," he said. "No. Please." She gave no sign of having heard him. He changed tactics. "Fuck you, bitch," he said. Again she gave no sign. Now she was pushing his head about, roughly but without malice, as if his head were something inanimate that belonged to her. She pressed the phone into his head. He heard a ring. Two more rings and he was listening to his wife's voice on their answering machine. The image of her came to him through his terror, through his blindfolded eyes, and her scent and moods transported him away until he felt all the colors of regret and shame that he had so carefully tried to put away from himself, to be with this woman.

"I'm sorry," she whispered, close to his ear.

"Please leave a message at the tone," said his wife.

"Say darling," she said, in a louder voice now, commanding him.

Another jab at his throat when he was too slow to answer.

"Darling," he said.

"Say honey, hon," she said.

"Honey. Hon."

"Say, I don't know when we'll see each other again."

He parroted her words into the phone. His wife. His dull wife. All lost. She would lose him in more ways than one. A blessing that she had not answered the phone, at least. A blessing. Too good a sleeper. Too accustomed to strange late-night ringings from those who would remember them from the other side of the globe, whom they would rather forget.

"Say I love you," she said.

"I love you."

"Say, 'Always remember that, no matter what happens.'"

"Always remember that, no matter what happens."

"Good."

He heard the phone clatter on the nightstand. It began to ring again, almost immediately, a metallic sound that he heard from far away. The ringing stopped. Then she was on him again, flattening him into the bed, the wires on his wrists digging into his back, but most of all he felt the pressure of that sharp thing at his throat, as if it were the single point that connected him still with the world. And he thought, so be it. His mouth filled with the taste of old coins. I will keep my eyes open, he thought, even though they are in back of this blind. I will be Muslim. He waited. Her breasts heaved against his back with the exertion of her breathing. The pressure on his throat increased and he knew it was the end of him. And then, a miracle, he felt the woman give it up, felt the miracle of her choosing not to harm him, and now she was cursing him from somewhere further off, not next to his throat any longer, and she was crying, and whipping him across the back with sharp, stinging blows that he hardly felt because he understood deeply that some crisis had passed and that he had been spared.

At last, she stopped striking at him. He could hear her breathing in deep, shuddering gasps.

"Now you understand me," she said, dully, next to his ear. "Now we are together."

He felt her sigh.

He hated her.

She surprised him once more, by releasing his bonds, beginning with his feet, then his hands, then the blind over his eyes. She looked at him, puzzled, as if expecting to find someone else; and when he simply lay there, unable to throttle her as he wanted to, or even to look at her looking at him, she kissed his chest apologetically, then his abdomen, and finally took his cock inside her mouth with such gentleness that he felt as powerless and humiliated as before she had untied him. His wrists were striated from their bonds until they no longer felt a part of him; they had become all pulse; all throbbing, painful pulse. And yet his will to resist her lay shattered. He was aware of her soft hair, a little damp, touching him as her lips and mouth encircled him. She moved gently. He felt oddly beloved. To his wonder she made him come, and as he did so, he felt a confluence of selves rise up in him, where he was woman, man, victim, aggressor, Muslim, Jew, husband, wife all at once, and his head was filled with a dazzling light, before she rolled away from him, gagging and weeping, and he was alone once more.

For a long time after there was nothing, anywhere in the world, but the sound of each heartbeat.

Then, slowly, a first thought intruded itself. He thought again of his wife. The morning would come, as it always did, and she would wake and hear his voice on the tape, and she would hear this other woman with him, and there would be tears and consequences.

She lay apart from him, far across the bed, facing away and hunched together, her knees to her chest, so that the only part of her that he could see was the long curve of her spine.

25

She awoke to the sound of her husband's voice, and yet still was not entirely awake. She thought at first that he was standing next to their bed, speaking to her lovingly, home early from his trip. Or rather, he was in the kitchen, perhaps speaking with one of their daughters. Or he was somewhere in the house, on the telephone, a quick call to a business colleague before coming to bed and enfolding her in his arms.

When he didn't come she got up to look for him. She found her bathrobe in the dark and put it on, then padded barefoot through the silent house, past the slow, steady breathing of her sleeping daughters, to the answering machine in the kitchen, where she saw the blinking light, and knew that he wasn't home at all; that he had merely called her from far away. Three in the morning, she thought. A fine thing for him to be calling me at three in the morning. And forgave him even as she scolded him in her mind. Did she love him more when he was away? It was possible. When he wasn't with her, she felt less Persian. Less herself. He reminded her of who she was. She loved him, if only for that. She pressed the button.

"Darling," she heard him say. "Honey, hon. I don't know when we'll see each other again. I love you. Always remember that, no matter what happens."

Puzzled, not hearing correctly, she replayed the message. The words were the same. It was her husband's voice. What could it mean? It made no sense. It was impossible to understand him. He said that he loved her. But he didn't know when they would see each other again. There was something dreadfully final about it. She played the message again. His voice was strained. Cracked. Something. A kind of terror in his voice.

She played the message a fourth time. When it was done she found herself standing in a strange position, bent over the kitchen sink, clutching at its edge. For some reason she was staring at a damp dish towel, one that she could recall placing over the faucet to dry only hours before. My husband is in trouble, she thought.

This is an emergency. This is what an emergency feels like. I must stay calm.

She hastened to the bedroom where her daughters lay. Her girls slept peacefully. She closed the window in their room, which had been far too open, and locked it. She closed the door of the bedroom behind her and ran back to the kitchen, where she played the message again. This time when it was done she began to sneeze, then to cough. She bent forward, holding her face in her hands. She became aware that her hands were stroking her face. It was almost as if the hands belonged to someone else. To someone who was calm. To someone who knew what to do. The coughing stopped. The hands covered her face, gently, softly. She closed her eyes. She held her breath. The place behind her lids was profoundly dark. She took her hands away and opened her eyes and began to breathe again. She tried to remember what he had told her about his trip. Where was he? Boston? Washington? Wasn't he in Washington the week before? It must be Boston. She could call the police there. But the details of his trip were vague in her mind. She honestly could not remember the city. His secretary would know. But to call her now, at three in the morning, was it such a crisis as that? Could she be sure? She did not know what to do. Of course. She could call her husband back on his cell phone. The thought broke over her like water. Yes, she would call him back and just make sure that he was safe. She picked up the phone and called his number. The phone rang three, four times and she found an unbearable tension growing in her, trying to plan for the next few seconds, what to say, what kind of message to leave him in return, and she hung up quickly. Perhaps he couldn't answer. If he were in trouble, prevented somehow from answering his phone, then wouldn't it be better if it did not ring? A call from her could change things, if he were in some sort of trouble. It could change things for the worse. She would call the police. Yes. It was the right thing to do. If only she knew where he was. She began to doubt that he had ever told her. It was to have been such a short trip. Well then, could an operator trace his call? Yes. Operators did that sort of thing. Call the operator. She lifted the receiver and pressed zero.

She hung up again.

Impossible.

She played the message again.

"My husband is in terrible trouble," she said aloud.

She resolved to call the police in Boston after all. She would tell them that her husband was in terrible trouble. But saying the words aloud had left her with the understanding of how hollow they sounded. Who would believe her? What would she say to them? What details could she give? They would laugh at her. Or they would tell her to calm down. But she could not calm down. Because if she were calm, she might have to think of that dreadful possibility, that there was no emergency at all. She discovered that she was now walking in a small circle in the kitchen, as if pursuing that thought, and stopped short. She would not allow herself to think that far. The thought came, anyway, in spite of her efforts to defeat it: What if he was leaving

her? What would become of her then? That was it. It
was the only explanation for the words; for their final-
ity. He was not coming back. He had been behaving so
strangely lately. Hardly listening to her. Distant and
forgetful. A sudden temper about small things. She was
certain, now, that he had not told her his destination
before he had left. Why would he, if he weren't coming
back? She coughed. The irritation in her throat refused
to clear. She coughed once more, then took the hand-
kerchief from the pocket of her robe and wiped her
eyes. Wasn't it the most logical explanation, after all?

She played the message. This time, in the background, she heard what sounded like an echo, ghostly
and incorporeal, left over from some other message
and some other time. The echo sounded as if it were
parroting her husband's words. The illusion of repeti-
tion gave his words a solemnity that somehow comforted her. She was surprised to find herself crying. If
she were to call him now, he would hear a hysterical
woman. He would chide her for leaping to such fantas-
tic conclusions. Yes. She would call him again. But
what if he were leaving her? What good would a call
do? What if he were in trouble?

Her mind twisted away from either outcome and
she found herself thinking, inexplicably, of her husband's voice at another time, and of a conversation, so
long ago now, before their marriage. She had forgotten
that summer afternoon when they had sat together on
a hill, watching a rainstorm make its slow way up the
valley toward them. He had spoken to her of a friend
who had been killed. A boy who had been studying

aeronautics. He had gone on and on about it, in such gruesome detail that she had wondered what to make of him. She must have been thinking about the coming rain, and not really listening to him, at least at first. She could distinctly remember that she had been wearing her best dress, and thinking, as she watched the squall move closer, that she did not want to get the dress wet, and that it was probably already too late. Then something wonderful had happened. He kissed her. These many years later she felt again the sudden surprise of that kiss. Such an intimate gesture in public was foreign to them both, and always would be, no matter how many years they lived in this country. When he had finally let her go, he had told her. "I love you," he had said. "Always remember that. No matter what happens." She was sure of it. She could now remember it quite clearly. Precisely those words, delivered in just the same cadence as the message he had left on the machine. With just the same edge of romantic desperation. There, now. She understood at last. He had called to remind her of something precious, a memory they shared. She allowed herself to experience relief, then scolded herself for the way she had leapt to such rash conclusions. She would be angry with him, a little, when he came home, for leaving such an ambiguous message. He would tease her for not remembering right away. All would be well. And now she was very tired. Fatigue filled her senses to the same degree that anxiety had left them. But she felt quite incapable of going back to bed, almost as if to relax and lay her head down on her pillow might cause the anxiety to flow back into it. She resolved to get some air. She opened the front door and sat on the steps of their small porch, and waited for something to happen.

The sky was cloudless; the moon setting. She hugged her robe closer. The streetlight on the corner filled the night air with a rusty glow and made the air seem warmer than it really was. The same moon is setting over his head, she thought, then smiled at herself, because of course it was daylight where he was, because he was in Boston or Washington, getting on a plane somewhere on the East Coast, or was about to, or at least was waiting at the airport for what was evidently going to be some sort of delay, because that is what he had told her on the phone, that is why he had telephoned in the first place, so that she wouldn't worry. No doubt he was boarding a plane just now. That was why he couldn't answer his phone. But why had he chosen to leave the message for her in English instead of their native language, the language that they always used with one another? They would have spoken their own language to one another, that afternoon on the hill. Not English. And without warning the memory itself began to fall apart. Had she actually been wearing her best dress? Had they sat on a hill? Had he, in fact, kissed her? No. She did not want to think about it any longer. He had spoken in English because he had been with someone when he left the message. With a business colleague. He hated to give anyone the impression he had secrets, by speaking in a language they couldn't understand. That was it. Only when she had succeeded in convincing herself that all was well did her body stop its compulsive rocking back and forth. But she did not leave the porch. She sat there, completely still, until daybreak, when a car went by: a neighbor on his daily commute. He waved at her as he passed and she remembered that she was wearing nothing but her bathrobe and nightgown. She went back inside, turned the dead bolt behind her, and waited by the phone.

26

She lay on the bed and watched the sea-dawn, dank and cold, seep into the room from its edges. A dull light began to play at the corners of the curtains. Their long night was over. She discovered, only slowly, that the rising sun had turned her to stone. She was immobile. She lay with her head on his chest, the same as ever. She held the razor blade in her hands, the same as ever. But she understood now that she could not raise it again to skin. The will to hurt had left her and she wanted nothing more than to be simple again. Was it too much to ask? Was it really too much? To go back to the way other people lived, the lucky ones, for whom the illusion of a normal life was still reality? A lot of things hurt inside of her. Perhaps the coming day would inspire her to discover why. She possessed a certain level of self-knowledge now, she reminded herself, of which she could be proud. Time had passed and her experiences had grown deeper if not more coherent.

Alternatively she wished for a disaster, like the ones they had imagined for one another the night before; a pox, a plague, a pure, holy terror event after which all that had come before would be erased in a brilliant white light, rendered irrelevant from one searing moment to the next, so that all the world could experience the same dislocation that she had. The shattered pieces would rearrange themselves eventually. Life would go on. But no one would return to the before-place, when everything was ordered and complete. In this way they would all be equal, just as this man lying next to her had become her equal. She prayed fervently for great crumblings of civilization all around them. How much better for them both.

A whisper of a thought traveled through her mind and she snatched at it as it passed, a feeling that she imagined might be hope for the future. After all, he had been very kind to her. A gentleman. He had worn cologne for her. And he could hardly go home now. Not after what they had shared together. A vast tenderness washed over her as she thought of his words of love, of the cologne, until it erased his transgressions, and she forgave him, and she became flesh, not stone, once more.

He had slumbered off again. The simple ordinari-
ness of his light snores moved her. Gently, so not to
wake him, she kissed him. He made no move. He was
very dear to her now, very precious. "How lovely," she
murmured.

She folded herself under his arm and covered them
both with sheet and blanket, and laid her head on his
chest, where it felt as if it might belong.

27

He awoke, but did not open his eyes. A woman was sleeping on him, curled into him, her breath steady and warm on his shoulder. He didn't move. He made no alteration in his breathing. He kept his eyes tightly closed, consumed by one thought: If only I could open my eyes and see it is my wife curled into me in this intimate way. He had little hope for her forgiveness. He had no choice but to pray that she would be restored to him by a supernatural event, such as appearing by his side in this bed. If he were faithful enough, the next moments in his life might resolve themselves in just that way: his own bed, her head on his shoulder. He opened his eyes. It was not his wife, of course.

Unable to stop himself, defeated by his own weakness, he lifted the coverings, just as he had the afternoon before, to look at her as she slept. What he saw was an alarming amount of blood, which caused him to sit up, no longer mindful of her head on his chest, and to touch himself all over. Her head fell onto the bed next to him. He discovered that his skin was relatively intact, except for the wrists, which were stripped bare of skin and oozing a viscous substance that was tinged with pink. He touched his neck and found the wounds there had already closed. Had she cut herself, then? He examined her more closely as she lay next to him. There was only the smallest of marks on her, scratches about her throat and arms. The insignificance of their wounds amazed him. It dawned on him that it must be her menstrual blood. Now that he had identified it, the odor became familiar and reassuring, and an odd sense of victory overcame his disgust. But he did not want to touch her.

It was then that her fingers opened and closed in sleep. A brief spasm, and then it was gone. He watched the fingers, unable to help himself, feeling himself invaded by her once more. That brief, spastic movement of her blood-covered fingers imprinted itself on his mind, and he knew that he would never again remember with complete accuracy the one thing he was certain of in the death of his friend, which was the way his friend's fingers had opened and closed in the dirt. He would think of this woman's fingers instead. And so his friend now was entirely forgotten. A deep sense of loss overtook him, followed by what he could only describe as relief, followed by the obscure certainty that his purpose in coming to meet this woman had now, at this very moment, been fulfilled.

He stood stiffly and walked to the bathroom, where he relieved his bladder and washed away the blood. He looked in the mirror and touched his throat and wondered at how a wound so insignificant could have caused him to fear for his life. The marks on his back, so biting and cruel at the time of their creation, had resolved into a rash of scabbed-over marks that itched but did not pain him. His only worry was that the scabs would fall off during the long ride home and leave his shirt streaked with new blood. He would need to be careful.

The wrists were another matter. There were places on each wrist where his skin was rubbed away entirely, and there were narrow, painful trenches grooved into the skin below the base of each thumb, across the bone. He washed frantically, praying the marks would simply disappear, wringing the cloth out and filling it with clean water, over and over again, letting the hot water pour over his wounds until they felt purified. He tore strips from a towel and tied them around each wrist with his teeth. He was deeply troubled by the thought that the wounds wouldn't close before he got home. That they would bleed through onto his shirt and he would need to explain to his wife, right away, and she would say to him, Good God, Changiz, what have you done to yourself? The thought of his wife like that, running out to meet him, full of concern, full of love, filled him with grateful wonder. To think of her saying his name aloud, to think of her calling his name in this way, with love in her voice. But what could he reply?

He walked softly back into the bedroom. She slept on. He would fear for her if it weren't for the steady breathing, the look of peace. He turned his attention to his valise, unzipping it slowly, not wanting the noise to awaken her, wanting nothing more than to get away from her before she woke up. He dressed quickly in his one pair of clean trousers, his one clean shirt, and stuffed the other things away inside the valise. His sleeves covered the makeshift bandages around his wrists. Good. He zipped the valise again. As he did so, he thought about writing her a note. He had no desire to awaken her. But a note. It felt correct to write something, after what they had been through together. But what was left to be said? There was nothing more to be said. He needed to get out of there and never see her again. Not one moment longer. Then he recalled that he would need money for fuel, and set to looking about for her purse, searching about with increasing anxiety on the floor and bed until he found it on the chair at the writing desk in the corner of the room. He took out the billfold and helped himself to three twenty-dollar bills. He would send her back the money at some point. But he might need more. Only the morning before he had paid a hundred dollars for five gallons, after all. He emptied the billfold. He took it all. She had the credit cards still. She could telephone her friends for help if she needed it, something he wasn't in a position to do. At the last moment the look of the empty billfold called to him and he put back one of the twenties, stuffing the rest into his trouser pocket without counting it. There. He was ready. He would go home. He would find a way home again. His eyes fell on her and he was dismayed to find hers were open; she was watching him.

"Look, I took some money," he said. He felt his face grow hot. "I'll pay you back, of course."

She said nothing. A terrible weight of obligation settled on his shoulders, rooting him to the spot. Now that she was awake, now that she had seen him take her money from her billfold, he found it awkward to simply walk out the door. He wanted to avoid touching her again, however. She would expect him to touch her again. She had paid him off, in a way, to touch her again.

"You're angry with me," she said.

"Of course."

"Come sit over here. On the bed."

He didn't move.

"Please."

She looked at him, the blankets over her, her knees drawn up to her chin.

"You disgust me," he said.

"You'll never forgive me, I know," she said. "You're disgusted with me. Go away now, if you want. I understand."

He sat down on the edge of the bed, by her feet.

"Last night feels like a dream," she said. "A dream that leaves in its wake only a great tenderness. That's what I feel for you, you know. A great tenderness. I wonder if you can understand that."

He looked at her, incredulous.

"No," he said. "No, I can't really imagine it."

"That's because you've already forgotten your part in things," she said. "It's the way we are. We order the past to suit our image of ourselves. It works as long as everyone around you cooperates."

"I need to think about going," he said. "I have a long drive ahead of me."

"It's terrible, how we forget," she said. "I used to think it was very sad how when we die all our memories die with us. Now I realize the memories die long before. Even our most beloved memories. Our most horrifying memories. I'm terrified at the way I keep disappearing."

"I suppose," he said.

He wanted to walk to the curtain and open it, to see those wretched patio chairs once more and to verify with his own eyes that the light bleeding in from its edges was indeed coming from the sun. To think he had allowed her such liberties.

"You are too extreme," he said. "It isn't good for you."

A sound came, the rush of water through pipes, re-assuring in its own strange way. People were about. Be-having normally. Flushing toilets. He noticed that his hand was tapping rhythmically on his knee as he sat there. A nervous habit that comforted him.

"Tell me what happened to you in Tehran," she said.

"That? What could you need to know about it?"

"Please," she said.

"I was in a crowd," he said.

Tell her then. But simply. Without emotion. A way to punish her for her monstrous, egotistical grief.

"Everyone I knew was there," he said. "We were students. We were carrying signs. Death to the shah. Death to America. That sort of thing. My friend was shot through the throat."

He heard his voice change as he spoke, from calm detachment to something different, a catch in it, and he hated her for hearing it.

"You loved him," she said. Her voice was strangely calm and flat. "You still love him. There was blood. You screamed and fell on him and cried out his name."

"That's not the way it was."

"Of course not," she said. "Nothing is the way it was."

"No one counted the bodies," he said. "No journalists or monuments or speeches. Not like you Americans with your whining and your videotape."

"You're lucky," she said.

"Yes. Lucky."

Surprising himself, he watched his hand move until it was covering hers. He gave it a friendly if dispassionate squeeze.

"I'll never forget you," he said.

"You already have."

She took her hand away.

Rebuffed, annoyed by her lack of cooperation, he stood. Her arms reached up to him, pulling him down, and she kissed him on the mouth. He felt her fumble with the zipper on his pants, so quickly, so quickly, so unseemly! Let her, he thought. He had nothing left to lose. Then, sickened by his lack of discipline, he pushed her back onto the bed and stepped back. His one clean shirt.

"No," he said.

He moved out of her reach and grabbed up his things.

"Do you still think I'm beautiful?"

He looked at her, fragile, no longer a threat, no longer groping his privates. He could do that for her.

"Yes," he said.

A pause then, a balance, where he felt as if he might fall one way or the other, to hold her or to strike her. She looked ready to be beaten. Eager for it. But no. He looked away from her for the last time, and left.

Once outside the door he began to walk briskly down the carpeted hallway, then broke into what was almost a run, scooting along with his valise bumping at his shins. The route back to the lobby felt longer than he remembered. Numbers on the doors of the rooms rose and fell and rose again. He imagined her running behind, tracking his scent. She had sprung up from their bed and was now running after him, crying out: come back, come back! He saw her silhouette in the dimness at the end of one hallway and stopped still with fear, before running away again. The shape did not call to him. Perhaps it was someone else, a ghost. Or no one. A fire extinguisher. To his surprise he found himself in the lobby.

The man was behind the desk again, spinning on his stool, the very one who had recommended a restaurant in town to him the night before. He felt a moment's dislocation before rage and indignation filled him.

"Look here," he said, startled at how commanding his voice sounded. "What did you mean, sending me to that restaurant of yours?"

The man on the stool looked bewildered.

"It's the best place in town," he said.

"The best place in town! I had to run out of there before I was beaten up."

The man's face arranged itself into an expression of such deep shock that it seemed artificial, a sham. A vivid certainty coursed through him, that this man had set him up, that this man was somehow responsible.

"Yes. I had to run out of there, leaving my billfold behind. You needn't look so shocked," he said.

"But that's terrible," the man said. "Oh no. No, no. We'll call the police."

"That's quite all right," he said. "I'll take care of it."

"You'll take care of it?"

"Yes. I'll take care of it."

"Well then," the man behind the desk said.

He looked lost for a moment, searching for what to say next; then his features relaxed. "How was your stay with us?" the man said.

The man's face had now taken on the obsequious, mock-friendly air of someone in the service industry. Perhaps he could ask him for help. Proper bandages, for instance. But he was reluctant to reveal his needs to this particular man, or to anyone else for that matter. At any rate it would be impossible to explain. If anything at all could ever be explained.

"Fine," he said. "Very fine. Thank you."

He hesitated, then continued.

"There is a woman in the room," he said. "She will be coming out later. You are not to disturb her until she is ready to leave. Is that all right?"

He took one of her twenties out of his pocket and placed it on the counter.

"Yes sir," the man said. "She'll be all right. Checkout time isn't until noon."

He looked at the man on the stool. Had he done enough for her? Of course he had done enough for her. More than any man could be expected to do. He felt awash with the righteousness of his actions. He took his car keys from his pocket and felt the weight of them, gratefully, as he walked out to his car, the valise swinging freely in his other hand. The sun still shone down brightly from the sky, the same as ever. He unlocked the trunk and threw the valise in. He got into his car and sat for a moment and savored his solitude.

He turned the engine over and let it idle as he searched under his seat for his music. The sound of it comforted him. All would be well. As he drove away he felt as if his skin were returning, layer by layer, and knew that soon he would be himself again. He needed to believe it. After a while, he realized that he was thinking of his childhood, before he had become so hopelessly Westernized, before he had become so much a part of this culture that he could hardly find himself in it any longer. His mother had cooked on a small burner on the floor of their kitchen. She had preferred her feet to be bare. Every night his father had listened to his son recite the Koran. His sisters had bathed him when he was young. From the flat roof of their house as a child he could hear the sounds of buses and traffic and children in the school yard a few blocks away. He snatched at these small threads of memory as if they were his last, most desperate hope to find himself. His back was aflame with an itching so intense that he wanted to stop the car and claw at himself until it stopped. Every time he thought of her a wave of disgust rose up in him until he thought that he must drown from it. But he did not drown. He did not stop. And as the miles passed and he left her and the memory of her behind him he began to feel at ease again. After all, it had been her own confused desires that had been the problem. Not his. How was he to know? He had tried to be kind to her. He drove back to the restaurant to inquire about his wallet and found it locked. He would call them later, from the road. His billfold would be returned. All would be well. A hundred miles later and he began to stop worrying about the past, and instead imagined the future he was driving toward: his wife, his home, the man he had been. What could he possibly tell his wife? What could he ever say to her? By the time the road turned east a plausible lie had come to him. By the time he reached his home he almost believed it.

28

After he left her she felt less sad than she had supposed. But she wanted to feel sad. She wanted to feel the grief of separation again. She lay on the bed and willed herself to feel it, but found instead that her thoughts kept interrupting themselves, until her will to grieve was overridden entirely by a buoyant sense of release. It could be, she thought, that her ability to grieve had become so depleted that it had no hope of renewal. Like the passenger pigeon, she thought. Things get to a certain point beyond which the whole system collapses and disappears. She had read about that sort of thing.

It occurred to her slowly that she wanted to cleanse herself. In the shower she wondered dully about flowing things. Water. Time. Blood. Flow. A funny word for it. Small clots of blood were falling out of her, sticking along her legs. She scrubbed until her skin was no longer hers. Then she stepped out of the shower, back into an empty room. Not wanting to lose again the precious feeling of civilization and cleanliness, she unzipped one of her bags and rummaged about in the pockets until she found a stash of sanitary products. She noticed that there were also many clothes in her suitcase as well, of different sorts and styles. Really, she could be anyone today. Slut. Librarian. Overwhelmed by the weight of choice, she sat down naked in the chair at the writing desk. She longed for a cigarette, although she had never smoked. She opened the drawer, took out the letter she had written on the night she had arrived, found a pen, and began again.

"Darling," she wrote.

"My intentions have become a mystery to me. Too much thinking on the subject leads me into treacherous waters. I have become a great sea turtle, plumbing the depths of distant darks but on land barely able to struggle forward, inch by inch. I will never be able to forget you. I will never be able to forget that I am your widow. I find myself drowning in the moment of our last sorrow together. Over and over again. You would tell me to move on. I do try. Yet I find myself back again, back at that first, horrifying moment when I knew that you would not be returning to me. My life has become a series of ceaseless, glittering turnings back to that moment. Everyone else moves on, away from me, decision upon decision, act upon act, until I'm left all alone with you. Hon. I want to tell you something. I met with a man yesterday. We made love. Now he has moved on. Our time here together is already growing dim in his mind, and I find myself all alone here with you again, back where we began, while he is running home with my cash in his pocket, running home as fast as he can, home to his wife, so that she can remind him of who he is, remind him over and over again, before he gets left behind."

She put the pen down, then picked it up.

"There you have it," she wrote.

She put the pen down.

She went to the bed and stripped it and gathered the sheets into a great wad on the floor, arranging them so that the stains would be less noticeable. I must leave a tip, she thought. A difficult job, cleaning hotel rooms. She gathered up the towels and added them to the pile on the floor. While doing so she discovered her bra. Oh, here you are again, she thought, and put it on. She walked to the closet and found her blue suit, a favorite of hers. The skirt was soiled. She dabbed at it with a wet tissue until it satisfied her. The blouse was also soiled, a long yellow stain just below the collar, so she buttoned the jacket of her suit to make it less noticeable. The hose were hopelessly ruined, pulled apart with great rents in the legs by the crotch. She dressed herself with as much care as possible under the circumstances. She decided to put her shoes on without hose. Her legs were recently shaven. It would not look so inappropriate. She ran her fingers through her hair. All would be well. She took the last twenty-dollar bill out of her purse and left it on the table, under the key. She stuffed her writings into her purse and closed it. She looked at her bags for a moment. Then she walked to the door, opened it, and left the room.

A few minutes later she found herself standing at the top of the iron staircase where it clung to the cliff. Here was where they had met. What had she come for? What had she expected from him? Resolution. Explanation. Understanding. She fell to looking for the right word in her mind. She knew that she would never find it. So she stopped looking inside herself, and looked out at the waves instead, and thought of all the possibilities open to her in the future. She could fly away to meet her end. Or she could follow him home. Find a way to be with him. They had been through so much together. To be his rough whore and let him slap her whenever he desired it, to make up for what she had done to him. She could persuade him. He had a weakness. Alternatively, she could stay. Stay right here in town. What would it be? What would it be? She clutched at the rail, then let go and stood unsupported. She felt the wind grab at her. To appease it she took the two letters she had written from her purse and ripped them, methodically, into tiny pieces, until in a sudden gesture she threw them over the side, where they were instantly carried up, high above her head, and flew away.

Feeling lighter in spirit, she looked down the beach, toward the town, searching for answers. Soon, in the distance, she saw a woman in a blood-red scarf running laboriously through the sand in her direction. Why, that's me, she thought, that's me; I'm running through the sand. I will run to the top of these very stairs, just as I ran through the sand yesterday morning. This time I will wait for myself. This time I will be calm. I will wait for her calmly, here at the top of these stairs, and when she reaches me, I will embrace her.